# BLOOD THIEF

## MICAH REED BOOK 3

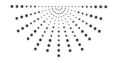

## JIM HESKETT

# OFFER

---

Want to get the Micah Reed prequel novel **Airbag Scars** for FREE? It's not available for sale **anywhere**. Check out www.jimheskett.com for this free, full-length thriller.

Also, read on after the main text for some fun, behind-the-scenes extras.

---

*Gonna shake hands around the world*
    *Down by the riverside*
    *I ain't gonna study war no more*
    *Study war no more*
    *Ain't gonna study war no more*

— TRADITIONAL

# PART I

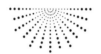

MEMORIES OF GOLD WATCHES

# CHAPTER ONE

W HEN FRANK LIFTED the cover from the cake, Micah Reed burst out laughing, but probably not for the reasons Frank had intended. White frosting topped the cake, with a single candle and an icing picture of some blueish blob thingy with gray streaks running through it.

A lake, maybe, or a swimming pool? Micah couldn't figure it out.

"What's so damn funny?" Frank said as he hefted the cake onto Micah's desk.

"Well, it's just… I mean, I appreciate you getting me a cake for my one year and all, but I have no idea what that is supposed to be. Is it like an abstract thing?"

Frank huffed a sigh and retreated into their office's kitchen to grab a coffee mug. Micah worried for a second that he might have pissed off his boss, but Frank returned a moment later, with no anger written on his wrinkly face.

Frank craned his neck, squinted at the blue blob. "Well,

crap. It's supposed to be a bird escaping a cage, you know, symbolism and all that. I asked the girl at Whole Foods if she could do a bird, and she said it was no problem. Looks like she oversold her talents."

Micah stroked an imaginary goatee. "Ahh, I get it now. Symbolism. One year sober, free of the cage of alcoholism. That's clever, Frank. Real clever."

Frank shook his head. "Yeah, yeah, kid. This is about as sentimental as you're going to get from me today. Cut yourself a piece and let's get back to work."

Micah picked up the knife and was preparing to dig into the cake, but he stopped himself. Maybe Frank wouldn't want to hear it, but Micah needed to say it. "I mean it, though. I'm not exaggerating when I say I'd be dead in a gutter if it weren't for you."

"That's how it works. I sponsor you, and if you don't relapse, you eventually go out and sponsor other people."

"Like a Ponzi scheme but with good intentions instead of lies and bankruptcy."

This time, Frank did grin. "You got it. You're a year sober, so it's about time you started expanding your horizons."

The knife slipped into the cake, and Micah sectioned off a corner for himself. "My horizons, eh? That brings up a good point. For the last year, I've been thinking about not much besides getting twelve whole months under my belt. Stringing together as many days as I could."

"And?" Frank said.

"Now I've got a year. So what do I do with myself?"

"Mostly, you keep living one day at a time. But it's also

time to start figuring out what you want to be when you grow up. Go out into the world and mix with the normal people. Make a friend. Write your memoirs. Take a pottery class, or whatever. Doesn't matter, as long as you keep doing what's required to stay sober on a daily basis."

*Make a friend.* Not an easy task for Micah, for more than a few reasons. Not the least of which was that his name wasn't actually Micah Reed. Not the name he'd been born with, anyway. He'd had plenty of experience reciting the version of his past that included all the government-approved fake details, but it never got any easier.

Before he had time to dwell on this further, the door at the front of Mueller Bail Enforcement opened, and in slinked a terribly familiar woman.

Dark skin, dark eyes, long dark hair. Wearing a t-shirt and jeans, which might have seemed strange for October, but Denver weather could be like that. She had a constricted gait, as if she was trying to keep her frame from tearing apart as she crossed the room. With her arms held close to her body, her legs kept tight together as she walked. When she came to a stop, her knees pointed slightly inward.

Micah knew her, somehow, but he couldn't place it. Like seeing a recognizable actress in a movie, but her name dances barely outside of your memory. The not knowing drives you so crazy that you have to get on the internet and investigate.

Frank shot to his feet and waddled across the office. "Morning, ma'am. Can I help you?"

She pulled her purse a little closer to her chest. "Daisy Cortez. You are Mr. Mueller?"

"That's what they call me. What can we do for you?"

Daisy nodded at Frank, then her eyes darted in Micah's direction a few times. Unsteady, flashing glances. "Hi, Micah."

The hair on the back of Micah's neck spiked. She knew his name? "Hi. You gotta forgive me, but I don't... do I know you from somewhere?"

"Yes. We live in the same building. I'm on the second floor. We met in the elevator on the way to the manager's office, a couple months ago."

Now it all clicked into place. Both of them on their way to pick up packages. They'd even chatted for a couple minutes that day, and now he remembered all of it. She'd been new in the building, worked at a coffee shop, had a boyfriend named Mason or something like that.

Micah crossed the room to greet her. "Daisy. I'm so sorry I didn't remember."

"It's okay. We only talked a little."

But Micah did remember seeing her around elsewhere, in the parking garage, maybe once or twice in the lobby. An attractive woman, shy, often didn't make eye contact. Always in a rush to get somewhere.

"What can we do for you, Daisy?" Frank said.

Her eyes bounced back and forth between Micah and Frank. She hitched a tense breath and blew it out as she deflated like a balloon. "I need your help."

# CHAPTER TWO

MICAH WATCHED DAISY take a nibble of the birthday cake and then set the paper plate on his desk. She gave a sheepish grin as she plucked a dab of frosting from her lower lip. She plopped the finger in her mouth and then wiped it on her jeans.

At least she hadn't asked why they'd served birthday cake on a Monday morning. Micah wasn't publicly "out" to most people as an alcoholic. Especially not clients, or even potential clients. Frank didn't talk about it either, although he was into his third decade of sobriety. Was probably easier for him to keep it confidential.

"You understand, Ms. Cortez," Frank said, "that this isn't normally what we do. We're not private investigators, although I do employ them from time to time."

"I know," she said. "I looked you up online. You do bail bonds and some bounty hunter work."

Frank sipped his coffee. "Then can I ask why you're coming to us? If you think you're in danger, maybe we're not the best place to start."

She scooted the purse in her lap closer. "Because I can't go to the police, and I don't know if I trust private investigators. They all know the cops."

"But why can't you go to the police?" Micah said. She'd only told them bits and pieces of the story, in a jumbled, non-linear ramble of information.

She sighed. Daisy wore her anxiety like a shawl, her shoulders climbing and then sinking with each labored breath.

"Because that's who I saw him with. My boyfriend, Nathan. That's who the other people were in the room."

"Why don't you start from the beginning?" Frank said. "Tell us again what you saw, step by step."

She crossed her legs with a hurried movement. Inhaled a few times through pursed lips.

"I went over to Nathan's house last night at about eight. I wanted to surprise him. When I opened the door, he was with all those cops."

"Your boyfriend is a cop, too?" Micah said.

"No, he works in logistics. He just knows these guys, like old buddies. I know only one of them, but not his name. He is larger, you know, with a gut. Light brown hair, thick mustache. He's a police officer up in Boulder County. Anyway, they were in the living room, and all that cash was just sitting on the table. Piled up like someone had overturned a recycling bin. So much money. I wanted to ask what it was for, how they got all this money they were counting. His brother was there, his twin. He always hated me. Nathan's brother, I mean. But before I could say anything, they all looked at me, real angry, and Nathan made me leave the room. He grabbed my arm and dragged me out and they pushed all the money onto the floor so I couldn't see it. But I already saw it."

"Drugs," Micah said. "It's almost always drugs."

Her head dipped and she wouldn't meet his eyes. "It's not drugs. I would know if he was doing that. But whatever it is, I'm worried about him and what he might do. I don't want to believe he'll hurt me, but he does get angry sometimes. I've never seen him as angry as he was last night."

Frank sighed and gave Micah a glance. "Ms. Cortez, what is it you would like us to do?"

"I want you to find out what he was doing. If he's into something bad. Maybe it's not his fault. You could help him get away from these people if they're making him do things against his will."

Micah was no private investigator. His official title at Mueller Bail Enforcement was *skip tracer,* an unglamorous data analyst kind of job. Researching people online who didn't want to be found. Bail jumpers, deadbeat dads, insurance frauds. But if taking on her request meant simply spending a little time on the internet to dig up some info on the boyfriend, he could do that.

She held out her phone, showing a picture of a man with black hair and blue eyes. "This is him. His brother is almost an identical twin, but with brown eyes. It's the only way to tell them apart."

Frank tilted his head at Micah. "You know I'm leaving to do that thing. Tonight, or in the morning. I haven't decided yet."

Micah opened his notebook to a fresh page and scribbled some numbers. He tore it off and slid it across the desk to Daisy. "This is my per-hour charge for standard skip tracing. Since I'd be doing this without Frank's help, if I have to go into the field, there'll be additional charges. That's if I have any expenses."

Daisy skimmed the page, winced, but she eventually nodded. "I can find the money."

"Do you have somewhere you can stay tonight? Somewhere your boyfriend Nathan doesn't know about?"

"I don't think that's necessary."

Frank cleared his throat. "Might be a precaution you should consider taking anyway. But make sure Micah has a way to get in touch with you."

She wrote down a phone number and slid the notebook page across the desk to Micah. "I have friends he doesn't know. People from work."

"Okay, then," Micah said. They all stood, recited some terse goodbyes, and she gathered up her purse. Micah escorted her to the door. On the way out, she kept herself small and clustered together, like she was expecting part of her body to detach and tumble to the ground.

When Micah turned around, he found Frank giving him the stare down.

"What's that look for?"

"You sure you want to do this on your own, kid?"

"No, but she sounds like she needs the help. Doesn't take a psychologist to figure out she's scared of this Nathan guy."

Frank wrinkled his nose. "You know she's not telling us the whole story, though. You can't blame me for worrying about people coming in here off the street, given your... privacy situation."

"She lives in my building. Daisy's not a stranger."

"Doesn't mean she's on the up and up."

"Fair enough, Frank. I'm going to check her out, too."

Frank waved his hands in an hourglass shape and gave Micah a wry grin. "Yeah, I'll bet you are."

Micah actually felt himself blush. He hadn't even thought about Daisy that way. She'd made it quite clear when they'd met back in the elevator that she had a boyfriend. Micah had immediately placed her in the *unavailable* folder when she'd first uttered that word.

Frank crossed the room with his hands in his pockets, shuffling his feet. Standard *Frank Body Language 101* indicating the old man had something on his mind.

A few framed pictures and other items lined the yellowing walls, like the photo of Frank in his police uniform, grinning in front of a towering stack of seized cocaine bricks. Frank's framed Renault Robinson Award from the National Black Police Association. He lifted that frame and carried it back to his desk. Frank sat, beaming at the award. "Did I ever tell you about the day I decided to retire?"

"I don't think so."

Frank leaned back in his office chair and traced a finger around the award's wooden frame. "It was after I moved here and made detective, this was about five, six years ago, now. I had this perp, I'd arrested him for the murder of a prostitute. Stone-faced, impossible-to-crack kind of guy. Like the serial killers you see on the TV shows, more or less."

Frank let loose a barrage of coughs, and Micah waited patiently for him to continue.

"So, I grilled this guy for an hour or two, finally got him to admit he'd done it. Brutal, awful murder. He sliced her up, drained her blood into a collection of glass jars. One of the most gruesome scenes I've ever witnessed. Later, we found a big stash of these jars in his apartment, like sixty or seventy of the things, all full of blood. Some newspaper reporter nicknamed him *the blood thief.*"

"Catchy," Micah said.

"After he admitted to killing the hooker, I asked him why he did it. Just for my own curiosity, you know. And he looked me straight in the eye, and with this wicked grin, he said, 'because she loved it. They always love it.'"

"What a sick freak."

Frank frowned and set the frame on the desk. "What happened next was basically a blur. I found myself with my hands around his throat, slamming him against the wall. Took three of my guys to pull me off him, and when they did, it felt like waking up. I went back to my office, popped in a piece of nicotine gum, and wrote up my retirement letter right then and there. Got my cake and my watch two weeks later."

Frank held up his wrist and jiggled the gold watch.

"That's a hell of a story, boss. Why tell me this now?"

"Whatever you do," Frank said, "watch out for yourself. Don't you go piloting your ship into the rocks just because you hear the pretty voices singing."

~

*INSIDE WITSEC BLOG*
*POST DATED 10.14*

*As I mentioned in the last post, the Witness Protection Program began officially in 1971. It had been running for a few years before that, unofficially, in bits and pieces. Operating on a shoe-string budget to get the job done. Which was: hiding criminals who'd agreed to testify. Sometimes illegally hiding them.*

*That's how this program began, and even though laws were passed later to make it legit, it's always sort of been on the edges of what's legal, and straddling that line between what's wrong and what's right. That messy gray area where the end supposedly justifies the means.*

*Take a criminal and give him a new life? Give him a chance to start over fresh, to wipe the slate clean? WitSec members even get to erase their credit history. Like declaring bankruptcy without the messy after effects.*

*I wish I could do that.*

*The purpose of this blog is to explore and expose some truths about WitSec. I'm not some high-ranking government whistle-blower from the inside. I'm just a regular guy who's trying to let people know about this shadowy program. Bring it into the light.*

*And why is it shadowy? There's very little information about it on the internet. The US Marshals who oversee it would tell you that it's to protect the program, because if the info got out, it would put those people at risk.*

*But the people who would be at risk are people who it's hard to objectively say are "good" people. Often cold blooded killers. Why should they get a second chance at life? Why should the rest of us living around them have to remain in fear over what these criminals might do again, given the chance?*

*Over the next few days, I'm going to release a series of blog posts that detail how WitSec is just another example of government corruption. I'm going to name names, and I'm going to bring out the truth. You'll learn about real people, who they were, who they are now. What they did, and what they're still doing.*

*Please subscribe to this blog by entering your email address in the sidebar, and get the posts delivered right to your inbox. Or, be sure to visit back every couple of days for new posts. It's going to be a wild ride, but you need to see this.*

~

CHAPTER THREE

MICAH PULLED HIS baseball cap low and zipped up his jacket. Denver's October chill had set in, without warning, this afternoon. In a few days, it would snow for the first time this year. The thick, white flakes excited everyone at first, conjured up notions of waxing up the skis and building snowmen. But when those same flakes would fall next March or April, they wouldn't be so welcomed. By then, the whole of the city would groan whenever the forecast indicated more of the white stuff on its way.

But no snow today, only a bite to the air. The stinging cold from the metal bench under Micah's butt seeped up through his jeans. He slipped his gloveless hands into his pockets, fingering the little plastic head of a Boba Fett action figure. Boba had been Micah's constant companion since high school. A gift from Micah's father, whom he hadn't spoken to in years.

A father that thought he was dead, and for good

reason. If Michael McBriar's dad found out his son hadn't died in a car accident after testifying against the Sinaloa cartel, that would put his own life in danger.

In a way, Michael McBriar was dead. He was now Micah Reed.

And in Micah's pocket, that Boba Fett action figure had been joined by a metal one-year AA chip, shiny and new. Three hundred and sixty-five days without a drink. Micah tapped Boba's head against the chip, relishing the feeling of plastic on metal.

Across the courtyard was Novo coffee, and Micah kept his head down while he watched through the glass doors. Inside, Daisy Cortez poured milk into some espresso drink, then wiped her hands on a green apron. As she stirred the mug with a stick, light reflected off a shimmering crucifix on a chain around her neck.

This little barista was something of a mystery. Micah couldn't find any useful information about her online, other than her address and that she'd relocated here from New Mexico a decade ago. More recently, only some social media pictures of her and the boyfriend, Nathan. Nathan had a twin brother, and occasionally, the three of them appeared in the pictures together. The pictures were usually at dinner in someone's house or apartment. No drunken bar selfies. No pictures with any cops or anyone who fit Daisy's description of the chubby man with a mustache.

Often, long gaps occurred where she posted nothing at all. None of this seemed out of the ordinary or suspicious. Plenty of people took social media breaks or posted sporadically for extended periods of time. Micah himself had been on one of those hiatuses since moving to Denver. Except for him, it wasn't a break, it was a reality of his new life with a new name.

The only thing about her that struck him as odd was the condo in the building they shared in the LoDo area of town. Nathan actually owned her condo, which made sense, because no way could Daisy afford that place on a barista's salary. Micah himself only owned his condo because the federal government had bought it for him as part of the deal.

But Nathan also had a four bedroom house in Broomfield. Hilltop view of the mountains, cushy neighborhood, built within the last five years.

All of this information was easily accessible on the internet. What it didn't say was why Nathan would put his girlfriend up in this condo in downtown Denver. Whether or not Daisy was paying him rent on the place, Micah couldn't say.

Micah's phone buzzed. "Hello?"

"Hey, kid."

"What's shaking, boss?"

"I've decided I will hoof it up into the mountains in the morning," Frank said. "I think our bail jumper is going to make an appearance."

"Sounds good. Be safe up there, Frank."

"You sure you don't want to come with?"

Micah sighed, gave himself one last chance to reconsider. "I appreciate it. If it's okay with you, I want to see this damsel in distress business through."

"I thought you might. You vet her?"

"She's clean, Frank. Not much information about her, but I don't get the sense she's anything other than genuine. I'm not convinced I buy the cop angle, but she could have been confused about the other people she saw."

Frank sighed. "Listen to your gut, but let your head make some decisions, too. It might take me a couple days to get this jumper squared away if he tries to play hide and seek with me."

"I understand. If this gig wraps up quickly, I'll join you up in Summit County."

"You got a plan?"

"Not really. Follow the boyfriend, see if I can find out where the money came from. Find out if she's got any interest in protecting him."

"If you think she's setting you up…"

"I'm not saying that, but women in love do strange things sometimes. I wouldn't take it for granted."

Frank paused. "Whatever you do, watch your back. You've got a lot to lose, if you understand what I mean."

"Will do, bossman," Micah said before hanging up.

Daisy handed a mug to a woman waiting at the end of the counter. She offered the customer a bright smile, lighting up her face. She tugged at the crucifix on the chain, then lifted it to her lips and gave it a quick kiss.

Micah had wanted to find some reason to doubt Daisy; to find something suspect about her and write off her pleas for assistance.

But he couldn't, and that meant he had to help her.

CHAPTER FOUR

D AISY COMMANDED HER hands to stop shaking, but they wouldn't obey. Stuck in the parking garage underneath the condo building in downtown Denver. She refused to leave the safety of her car until she could stop acting like a terrified little girl.

The decision to leave had not come easily. All day she'd wrestled with it, thinking of the suitcase she'd packed, sitting there, next to her front door. Not knowing if fleeing was the right move or if it would make Nathan suspicious and angry.

And what he would do with that anger.

Maybe going to Micah for help had been a terrible mistake. But he seemed like a good choice, didn't he? Her neighbor and his boss Frank dealt with criminals all the time, plus they weren't police, so she shouldn't have to worry about Nathan finding out.

Not that she knew Micah well, or had any reason to trust him.

"Stop it," she said to her reflection in the rearview mirror. "Get ahold of yourself, Cortez. Stop being a baby. Go in there, get your suitcase, and leave. That's all you have to do."

And then, as if refusing a direct order, the tears threatened to spring from the corners of her eyes. She'd grown tired of this rollercoaster, tired of never knowing how she would feel from one minute to the next.

Screw it. If she couldn't wait for the rollercoaster to even out, then she'd have to walk it off. Daisy pulled off her Novo coffee apron and dropped it on the passenger seat. She strutted across the parking garage, her knee-high boots clacking on the concrete, the sound echoing from several directions. Like a drumstick on a snare drum in a concert hall.

Once she was in the elevator, the anxiety leveled to a numb throbbing. Felt a little more like herself, whatever that meant. Daisy hadn't felt like "herself" since she was thirteen or fourteen years old. Before everything started. Before her life got away from her.

She exited the elevator and her shoes sank into the cushy softness of her floor's carpeted hallway. Such a nice building, in every respect. When she came in through the lobby, she adored the smell of the flowers. Different varieties every week. Lily-of-the-valley gave her the most pleasure, gardenias her second favorite. For some reason, she couldn't stand daisies. Maybe because it would have been too obvious.

Daisy paused at her front door and sensed something was off. She rolled her shoulders a few times and told herself it was nothing, only that same tiny demon crouched on her shoulder, warning her that everything was about to fall apart.

But when she pushed open the door, she found the demon was right.

A head poked out from the kitchen. Nathan.

His sharp black hair and sharper blue eyes burned at her, but the smile on his lips brightened the lower half of his face. He stepped out into full view, wearing an orange Broncos apron over his button-down shirt and tie. Ladle in one hand and a box of pasta in the other.

"Hey, babe," he said. "You're home a little early. I was hoping to have dinner ready for you, but I need a few minutes."

She managed a meager smile, then lifted her hand in a half-hearted wave. Dropped her purse on the nightstand next to the front door.

Nathan gestured with the box of pasta to beckon her forward. She felt her feet moving toward him, but she didn't want to do it. Wanted to turn around and flee.

Did he know? He could have had any of his cop buddies tailing her, had them find out what she'd said at Micah's office that morning. She didn't think she'd been followed, but it's not like she had any experience looking for that kind of thing.

When she was close enough to touch, Nathan set the box of pasta and ladle on the kitchen counter, then he extended his arms for a hug. She folded into him, turned her face so he wouldn't see her tears. His grip was firm and tight, and she remembered the way it used to make her feel safe.

"I'm sorry," he said. "I was rude to you last night."

"It's okay," she said, the words spilling out like water from a tipped glass. "I shouldn't have surprised you like that."

He held her out at arm's length and gazed deeply into her eyes. For a second, she felt that thrill of lust at the sight of his bright eyes and the neatly trimmed beard lining his cheek.

She wanted to ask him the names of the people who'd been counting the money with him. Those cops. She couldn't remember any of their names, but there was no way to inconspicuously draw that info from him.

His eyes drifted down to the packed suitcase next to the couch, the one she'd neglected to take with her when she'd left for work earlier. A clear sign of mistrust, packed up and ready to go.

He had to know she was going to flee. He probably already knew which friend she was planning to stay with. Nathan had a way of stealing the truth from her, sometimes with nothing but a glance.

"I didn't think you were coming over," he said. "I mean, that's no excuse for how I behaved. I shouldn't have made you leave."

She tried to blink away the tears, to hide them. Nathan ran a finger along the underside of one of her eyes, catching a droplet. His smile seemed so warm and comforting. Maybe she was wrong about the whole thing. Maybe her paranoia was taking over.

"Truce?" he said. "I'm going to make a kielbasa and cabbage stew like mom used to make."

She nodded because she didn't think she could open her mouth without crying harder.

"How was your day? Did you make a meeting?"

She shook her head and gulped a jagged breath so she could speak. "No, I came right here after work."

He gave her shoulder a squeeze, a little harder than she would have liked. For a second, his smile faltered, and she saw malice in his eyes. A warning. *You shouldn't have seen what you did last night. You shouldn't have been there.*

Or, had she misread his expression? Thoughts swam in her head and she couldn't make sense of anything.

Without a word, he returned to the kitchen and turned up the heat under a pot of water. "Dinner in about fifteen minutes."

Now that his back was turned, she stumbled away from him, toward her bathroom. Closed the door behind her. In this enclosed space, the comfort of the close walls gave her some relief.

Daisy plucked a cotton ball from a glass jar and wiped dripping mascara from under her eyes. Her hand shook so badly that she smeared it, and had to use three more cotton balls to clean up her mess.

"Cortez," she whispered to her reflection. "Is this happening? Are you imagining this?"

And the reflection had no answer for her. Maybe this had been a huge mistake and she should walk out there and tell Nathan what she'd done today. She could explain that it had all been a misunderstanding, and she'd call

Frank Mueller's office first thing in the morning and tell them to cancel whatever they were going to do. Forget the whole thing and let her get back to living the oblivious life she craved.

That itch came, that burning under her skin to escape. Numb the pain. Make the world blurry so she didn't have to deal with it anymore.

She opened the cabinet under the sink and removed her prized possession, the monogrammed flask. She unscrewed the cap and sniffed, but it didn't smell like alcohol. Didn't smell like anything.

Daisy ran her finger over the raised monogrammed letters. Felt the reassurance of cold metal in her hands. She turned it over and over, letting the light bounce from the flask to her bathroom mirror.

How could she live like this?

"Babe?" came Nathan's voice from outside the door.

She nearly dropped the flask but managed to grab the cabinet door and shove it behind the shampoo bottles. Too loud. She was so hasty that she bumped her head on the edge of the sink.

When she raised back up, the world spun for a second and she worried she might pass out. Her hands found the lip of the counter and she steadied herself.

The door opened behind her.

"Daisy?"

The edges of her vision blurred, but she could see Nathan's face filling the middle. "Yes?"

"What are you doing in here?"

"Nothing."

He stepped closer, squinted at her forehead. "Did you hit your head? You have a red mark there."

"It's fine," she said as she angled her face away from him.

He put a finger under her chin to raise her face. "You know I don't like it when you hide things from me. You can say anything as long as you're honest."

"I had a bad day at work. Everyone kept treating me like a piece of rotten garbage today. I leaned down to get out a roll of toilet paper just now and bumped my head. But, like I said, it's fine."

Again, he offered her that smile she couldn't read. Loving, or devious. Maybe it was the same smile.

"You gotta be more careful," he said.

# CHAPTER FIVE

**M**ICAH RECLINED ON his couch, coffee in one hand, phone in the other. He scrolled through recent news, but couldn't care about much of it. This politician said that other politician lied, this company bought that company, this doctor said that doctor's research was bunk.

Any casual glance at the headlines made the world seem like an awful place.

He wanted to be the kind of person who could read the news in the morning with an unaffected attitude, but he couldn't seem to do it. In his first couple months of sobriety, reading the news made him angry. All that injustice in the world. He'd internalize the plight of some person or group who had been wronged, and then let it ruin the rest of his day.

Now, he found he didn't care. Or not that he didn't care about current events, but he couldn't find a way to apply it to his life. With a little sobriety under his belt, he understood exactly how powerless he was to change most things in the world.

It's not as if he could become an activist and risk having his face achieve public visibility. That would be a death sentence, and not only for him.

"Maybe caring about the news is a second-year sobriety task," Micah said to the severed head of the Boba Fett action figure, sitting on his coffee table.

Boba said nothing, and Micah narrowed his eyes at the miniature bounty hunter. "Don't look at me like that. What are *you* doing about all the world's evils?"

Still, Boba remained silent.

Micah dropped his phone on the couch next to him and stared out the window at the outline of the mountains to the west. Snow capped the peaks, but none of that had made its way to Denver yet. Across the room from Micah sat a pair of Rossignol ski boots, fresh out of the box. The handful of times Micah had been skiing previously, he'd rented. But this was supposed to be the winter that he would fully embrace the Colorado lifestyle and brave the I-70 traffic on weekends to log a few runs at the Summit County resorts. Maybe Vail, if he was feeling fancy.

Not this coming weekend, though, because he'd probably be knee-deep in researching Daisy's claims about Nathan.

He picked up his laptop to conduct some searches on Nathan Auerbach. Linking him to Daisy proved easy because she tagged him in any picture they appeared in together. People made hardly any effort to hide their tracks online.

Nathan and his brother Alec were both members of a country club, were avid golfers, and frequently attended car shows. After some digging, Micah eventually uncovered that they owned a timeshare in Steamboat Springs.

"How many properties do these rich assholes have?" Micah asked the room.

But, none of this digging turned up anything illegal. Nothing dubious or strange. Just a couple of playboy white guys with lots of money to burn.

As Micah set the laptop aside to rub his eyes, his phone buzzed. A text from one of the few people who knew his secret:

*Thought you should see this.*

Below that was a link to a blog. Micah clicked it and watched as elements popped onto the screen, including the title: *INSIDE WITSEC.*

This was a blog about Witness Protection, declaring it a corrupt organization that wasted taxpayer money to give hardened criminals the life they'd always wanted. Freedom, a new identity, a fresh start.

Micah's pulse quickened as he scrolled through recent posts. So much insider information here. He'd never seen anything like this before.

Micah could agree with some of the author's assertions. WitSec was flawed. It certainly did take some bad people and set them free, based on the theory that the results (putting high-level bad guys in jail) justified the methods (freeing lower-level killers and drug dealers). But it wasn't as if WitSec people led the good life. Always looking over your shoulder, having to erase your past and links to anyone you might care about.

Having to leave the dead behind, and pretend you weren't allowed to mourn for them. Like Pug. Thinking that name made Micah's teeth grit. His best friend, dead because of the fucking Sinaloa cartel.

Dead because of Micah.

As he clicked back through the site, something caught his interest. There weren't many posts on the blog yet, but yesterday's entry said that upcoming posts would expose several people in Witness Protection. Both their old names and their new names. Would out murders, rapists, white-collar criminals.

The hair on the back of Micah's neck stood at attention.

He scoured the blog for personal information about the author, but couldn't find anything. No byline on the posts, no contact page. He performed a *WhoIs* search for the website, but couldn't find any identifiable information about who had registered it. Someone who'd covered his tracks to remain anonymous.

A page rank search showed the website was reasonably popular and had been gaining popularity over time. People would see this. People would read it and share posts on social media. What if Micah found his own real name on this site someday, exposing him as a former employee of such a ruthless organization?

He wouldn't be able to do anything to stop it. Like the news, he had no power here.

Micah clicked the link on the site to subscribe to new posts by email, and he entered an anonymous email he used from time to time. Then he closed the site on his laptop because he had to let it go. Had to move on.

With a sigh, he returned to researching Nathan. Daisy's boyfriend lived in Broomfield, a suburb of Denver halfway between downtown and the edge of the mountains. His title was Logistics Manager, and he worked as a consultant for several companies around the Denver metro. His profile picture on Facebook showed a man with a square jaw, jet-black hair, and blue eyes. A five o'clock shadow that Micah guessed was perpetually in that neatly groomed status. Like the facial hair a romance novel cover model might wear.

After a quick search for average salaries for *Logistics Managers*, Micah did some math. It didn't seem that Nathan would be able to afford his own four-bedroom house in Broomfield plus the downtown condo—not to mention the Steamboat timeshare—on what he was making consulting. Even at the upper salary range, no way could he afford all of those mortgages.

One point in Daisy's favor. This guy was making extracurricular money, no doubt about that.

Nathan's brown-eyed twin brother Alec was something like a traveling salesman. Medical device sales, which Micah imagined could explain some of the extra money, but there was no evidence anywhere that Alec was contributing to Nathan's mortgages. No proof of them having any financial connection, other than the timeshare.

And then there was the cop angle. Daisy had said she'd

seen Nathan and Alec with some cops she'd recognized, but she couldn't recall any of their names. Only that one of them worked in Boulder, was chubby, and had a furry mustache.

Investigating police officers who may or may not be corrupt could land Micah in a world of hurt. Only a whiff of his involvement could lead to any manner of unpleasant endings. That was the most difficult to believe of Daisy's claims, and the most dangerous one for Micah to investigate.

No. Micah would keep his focus on Nathan Auerbach, and not dig in too deeply unless he had something solid to go on. Be like a leaf on a tree: waiting, watching, ready to drop if the opportunity presented itself.

CHAPTER SIX

FRANK SLOWED HIS car to change to the exit lane for Frisco. 90 miles from Denver, in the middle of Summit County. Home to Breckenridge and Keystone and a half hour from Vail. Fortunately, it was a month too early in the season for skiing, so Frank didn't have to wrestle with a million damn tourists trying to reach the slopes.

He wasn't here to ski, anyway. He was here to apprehend a bail jumper, haul him in, and ensure he'd take home the reward money. It's as if these damn hooligans didn't realize that every time a bondsman put up their bond, that bondsman was risking his business. They didn't care, only saw the selfish route.

But Frank understood self-centeredness. Twenty-five years ago, he'd been in the same boat. Not the criminal activities part. He related to selfishness because back then he'd been drinking, and everything was about finding a way to get more alcohol, no matter who it hurt. No matter who got in the way.

Sobriety had changed Frank in many ways, not the least of which was pride in his work. And that's why he was in Frisco, about to put himself at risk again.

Frank slowed to enter the parking lot of the Baymont Inn, a four-story rectangle off the highway, overlooking Lake Dillon. He considered the parking lot out front, the one out back, and the one off to the side. Despite his ankle feeling swollen already at this altitude, he opted for the far parking lot to the side.

No sense in letting Zaluski find some way to tie the car to Frank, even though the jumper wouldn't know Frank was after him. Surely Zaluski would suspect *someone* would be trying to bring him in, but he wouldn't know Frank's face.

Attention to the details had kept Frank safe so far.

So Frank parked and hobbled across the lot with his overnight bag, swollen ankles and all. Near the inn, the overpowering stink of Asian food flooded his nostrils. It had come from the restaurant attached to the inn. Frank lifted his sweater above his nose, not that it did much good.

He paused to check the outside of the hotel. Four stories, scant balconies on the third and fourth floors. No outside emergency exit stairs. He couldn't see the roof from here, but there had to be a way to access it. Not that Frank expected a roof chase or to have to leap from balcony to balcony, but it was always good to know the layout before venturing into the lion's den.

He stepped into the inn's lobby, a dimly-lit and bustling place with 1970s carpet straight out of *The Shining*. Probably some retro thing to attract the ironic young hipster crowd.

Frank was looking for Tomás Zaluski, an alleged drug trafficker who'd found himself pulled over for a missing tail light in the Denver suburb of Westminster. The arresting officer had located five pounds of marijuana under the spare tire in the trunk. Not a legendary amount, which is why Zaluski had been able to bond out, which gave him the opportunity to skip his court appearance. And that is why Frank found himself in the mountains, to apprehend the jumper and secure the reward.

One of the rare cases that Frank took on for another bail bondsman. He hadn't posted the guy's bail, was only trying to recover him for a cash reward. Get him, get the cash. Don't get him, get nothing.

Frank approached the hotel front desk and smiled at a young white woman behind the counter.

"Morning," she said. "Welcome to the Baymont. Do you have a reservation?"

There were a few ways Frank could play this. As a detective, all he had to do was flash his badge, which most people accepted as a master key to unlock anything in the world. He'd see this young woman's eyes light up, and she'd escort him upstairs without any further questions. But, people's perceptions of bail bondsmen and bounty hunters were a little fuzzier. He could show her ID, but she might not be clear about what she was required to do for him.

Besides, Frank didn't have a legal right to access the hotel room to wait for Zaluski. He could enter Zaluski's home, but he would need explicit permission from the hotel to apprehend him there. And, given that Zaluski was in a hotel and not at home, Frank had to assume that the drug trafficker knew this. And, if he knew this, he had to assume that maybe Zaluski had some kind of arrangement with people here at the front desk. Tipping him off if anyone came by, asking questions about him.

All this leading to the point that Frank being honest about his identity and why he was here might hinder his goal. So he had to invent a better way to find out which room was Zaluski's.

"Sir?"

"Yes. I'm looking for a room. Something on the top floor, if you have it available."

She clicked at the keys for a few seconds, then flashed her youthful grin at him. Frank paid cash, used an alias, and wrote down a fake license plate number. No reason for this hotel to run his plates that he could think of.

With his keycard in hand and only a small duffel bag slung over his shoulder, Frank rode the elevator to the second floor. He walked into a slim hallway that came to a point at one end. That same severe carpet running the length of the floor. You could get lost staring at those angular shapes.

Down the hallway, a young woman was dragging a toddler behind her. The little boy kept trying to grab at the shapes in the carpet, and the mother would snatch him up, pull him along, scold him. Frank waited until the mother had moved on and turned the corner at the end of the hall.

He unzipped his bag a little and wrapped a hand around a baton, one of the few relics he kept from his beat cop days. He gripped it but did not remove it from the bag.

He stopped at the first open door he could find and looked inside to find a plump Latino woman wiping dust from the side of a wardrobe. Salmon-colored maid outfit wrapped around her ample frame.

"Excuse me?"

The woman clutched her hands to her chest and nodded at him. "Yes?"

"Sorry to bother you, but I'm looking for a friend of mine. We were supposed to share a room here, but it seems he checked in first. White guy, long black hair, about my same height?"

She tilted her face, her jaw switching back and forth. Wasn't buying it. "You cannot call him?"

"He's not picking up his phone. He left me a message and said he was on the second floor, but I don't know which room. Does that description sound familiar to you?"

Her eyes darted back and forth, and Frank could see her getting worked up. He considered mentioning that he had no connection with Immigration, but he didn't want to assume.

"No, I do not know him. I'm very busy, please let me get back to work."

Frank frowned, but he didn't trouble the lady any further. When he continued down the hall, he noted a man in a suit leaning up against the wall. Huge guy, could have been some ex-Broncos linebacker or something. Gray bumps all over his cheeks and neck from a poor shaving job.

"Sir, do you need something?"

"Just looking for my room."

The linebacker wore a low-lidded suspicion as he approached Frank. "Can I see your room key?"

Frank held out the keycard, his other hand still gripping the baton in his bag. As he let go of the card, the guy's eyes flicked down to the hand inside Frank's bag. Frank let go of the baton and shifted the bag around, behind his body.

The man in the suit took out his phone and swiped the keycard along some card reader thing sticking out of the headphone jack.

"Your room is on the fourth floor, sir. This is two."

Frank laughed. "Oh, silly me. That's right, isn't it? Don't ever get old, kid. You'll forget your glasses sitting on top of your head."

The man smiled politely, not giving much ground. These people were a wary lot. Or maybe that was Frank reading too much into things.

"No problem, sir. Let me walk you to the elevator."

The man returned the card and escorted Frank back to the elevators. Once Frank was inside, the man leaned in and pressed the 4 button.

"Have a good day, sir."

The doors swished shut and Frank quickly jabbed the 3 button as the elevator whirred to life. These explorations were so much easier back in his cop days. No need for all this damn cloak and dagger. But, given how much bullshit Frank had been able to leave behind when he retired, it was a fair trade-off.

He kept thinking of the *blood thief* story he'd told Micah the day before. Frank would take hard-to-find bail jumpers over sicko killers, every time.

On the third floor, he resumed his grip on the baton, ready to smack Zaluski over the head if their paths happened to accidentally cross. A few doors on this floor were open, the sounds of multiple vacuum cleaners droning down the hallway.

Frank stopped at the first open door to find a woman in the same color of maid outfit holding a garbage bag in her hand. He opened his wallet and flashed his ID. "I need your help, ma'am."

She glanced at it, and Frank let her have about half a second before he shut his wallet and slipped it back in his pocket.

"What do you need?" she said. "I'm kinda busy here."

He ran through the description of Zaluski and his sad tale about not knowing where his friend was staying. The woman's face remained neutral as he spilled the story. She gave no hint of empathy or understanding.

When he'd finished, she said, "fifty bucks."

"Excuse me?"

"Come on. I don't buy your missed connection crap for a second. But I know the guy you're talking about, and I have a good idea why you want to find him. You want me to give you a master key to his room and also keep my mouth shut? That's gonna cost you fifty dollars."

Frank grumbled. Fifty dollars was gas money for the trip home, but as a going rate for information, it wasn't bad. Plus, he had a grudging respect for this woman's business savvy.

When he handed over the money, she slipped it into the pocket of her apron. Leaned her head toward the wall. "Two rooms down. 307. That guy is a nasty, nasty jerk. If you're here to arrest him, give him a couple licks for me, please?"

"I'll see what I can do."

With a master room keycard in hand, Frank soft-shoed it two doors down. He unzipped the bag and removed the baton, then dropped the bag on the floor behind him. Leaned close and heard something coming from the room, low volume. Could be a person talking on the phone or could be the TV. Could be two people in there, which gave Frank some pause.

Whatever was on the other side of that door, Frank would have to open it to find out.

He raised the baton and swiped the keycard through the door.

# CHAPTER SEVEN

WHEN HE FOUND out Nathan Auerbach drove a sleek, late-model Aston Martin, Micah decided for sure that he didn't like Daisy's boyfriend. Maybe it was because Micah still drove the same battered Honda Accord he'd crashed into a ditch a little more than a year ago. Or maybe it was representative of something bigger about Nathan's character. His need to flaunt.

"Yeah, I know," Micah said to Boba Fett, whose head was sitting in the cup holder in the car. "I'm playing amateur psychologist a little too much lately. But you know what, Boba? A year of sobriety, maybe I'm entitled to think I know a little more about the human condition than I used to."

Boba Fett said nothing.

Micah had that shiny Aston Martin in his sights as he drove along I-270, headed east. There wasn't much out this way past Denver besides the airport and a few warehouses. Since Nathan worked in logistics consulting for different companies, maybe he was visiting one of those company's satellite locations. That would make sense since it wasn't yet lunch on a weekday. Micah hadn't found much clarification about the day to day responsibilities of a *Logistics Manager Consultant*.

When Nathan turned onto Peña Boulevard, Micah disregarded the warehouse theory. Denver International Airport had to be Nathan's destination. Or something near it. Micah kept his distance because closer to the airport, the traffic would thin to a trickle. Nathan could maneuver his Aston Martin between any straggling cars with laser efficiency. Micah had to work hard to keep up, but not look like he was keeping up.

Best to stay unnoticed. If this guy liked to spend his free time counting possibly illicit cash with possibly corrupt cops, who knew how paranoid he was.

Or dangerous.

Or, maybe not dangerous at all. Maybe just a rich boy with flashy cars and houses and a girlfriend who jumped to conclusions. This whole thing could be in Daisy's imagination. That's what Micah was here to find out.

Nathan exited off Peña at 75th, about a mile before the airport. This was rental car and private hangar territory, and as Micah suspected, Nathan slowed and turned into a lot with a small airfield and a collection of hangars. Those enormous metal buildings with no decorations.

Micah continued along 75th, keeping Nathan in his rearview to see which hangar he'd stopped at. Micah pulled a u-turn at the next opportunity, as two other cars came to a stop next to Nathan's in the parking lot. A BMW and a sporty thing that might have been a Lamborghini. Micah wasn't a car expert.

Whatever kind of car it was, this collection would have been any rich guy's wet automotive dream. Micah didn't understand the need to drive something so expensive. As long as his car worked, that was good enough for him.

As Micah neared the hangar, he piloted into the gas station across the street and idled at a pump. He reclined his seat to get a decent view without exposing himself as a gawker.

Nathan stepped out of his car and his brother Alec emerged from the BMW. They looked exactly alike, right down to the haircut. Micah wouldn't be able to tell them apart in a lineup, that was for sure. Then, he remembered Daisy had said that Alec had brown eyes, not blue like Nathan.

Some other man stepped out from the Lamborghini. The new man looked like an Eastern European gangster. Slim, tall, tweaker-short hair, big aviator sunglasses. Something familiar about him gave Micah that same sense of unease as when he couldn't remember where he'd seen Daisy before. Not likely that this guy lived in Micah's building too, but Micah knew his face.

All three of them sported razor-sharp suits. Micah raised his phone and snapped a few pics of the three of them. He was too far away to get clear face shots, but he might spot something useful in these photos, anyway.

The three men stood in front of their cars, legs spread

wide and hands clasped in front of their waists. Eyes forward, not speaking. They were waiting for someone.

A few seconds later, another car entered the lot. Not a luxury sports car, rather a big truck, with oversized tires and an extended cab. Micah didn't know the model.

The truck parked opposite the three luxury cars, and a nondescript man wearing normal-looking clothes got out. He faced off against Nathan and the other two. For a few moments, none of them spoke or made any movement to meet in the middle. A standoff. A tumbleweed might as well have crossed the pavement between them.

Daisy had suggested that her boyfriend Nathan wasn't into the drug business, but everything about this interaction screamed drug dealers. The fancy cars. The tailored suits. Nathan's multiple residences. Corrupt cops. It had to be drugs, didn't it?

The three fancy guys on one side and the regular guy on the other side talked for a couple minutes, but Micah had no idea what about. He couldn't read lips and he had no spy equipment to pick up their voices.

But after another minute, he didn't need sound to understand what was going on.

The nondescript guy approached the other three, his hands out. He was pleading. Nathan backhanded him across the face, then Alec grasped the guy by the arms and spun him. Now restrained, the European gangster loosed a barrage of punches into the guy's midsection. He made little attempt to slip free or fight back.

This lasted for fifteen or twenty seconds. Nathan took

his turn, cracking the man across the jaw a few times, until Micah could see the spatter of blood from here.

Eventually, it stopped, and they dragged the poor guy off toward the hangar. Blood dripping from his mouth fell in red dots, like breadcrumbs leading back to his truck.

Micah's voyeur episode came to a screeching halt when a car horn honked. He glanced around to find that all the available gas pumps were now taken. The horn honked again, and Micah checked his rearview to find some guy giving him the finger. *Get some gas or get out of my way, asshole.*

Micah lifted a hand to acknowledge the guy, then started his car.

## CHAPTER EIGHT

ICAH PARKED BEHIND the gas station and crossed the road on foot, aiming toward the hangar. He pulled his Denver Nuggets baseball cap low as he entered the same parking lot as the hangar. The building was an enormous barn-like structure with corrugated metal outside. One garage-type door for the plane entrance, which was currently closed. A couple of human-sized doors were at ground level.

A small plane roared and sped toward the ground, engines sputtering as it leveled off and descended. It matched the angle of the runway between the rows of hangars. Touched the ground once, twice, then skittered a little as it slowed near the end of the runway. Micah watched it come to a stop. Heat rose from the runway in waves of curved air.

Micah kept to the edge of the parking lot, walking as if he were trying to pass the hangar without directly crossing its path. Actually, he wanted to come close enough to see what kind of outdoor surveillance the building had. He would assume that Nathan, Alec, and the European gangster were busy pummeling that guy from the truck, but couldn't say there weren't others inside the hangar, watching security cameras.

There could be any number of things inside that building worth protecting. But Micah wouldn't learn what those things might be until he could get access.

Out of his peripheral, Micah did see a couple of cameras over the main hangar door. But, nothing pointed at the side doors, which gave him a ray of hope he could break in if given the chance. Maybe not today, but at some point. He had to see what was inside that hangar.

Once he had escaped the reach of the front cameras, he veered inward on a path that would take him to the back corner of the building. If the hangar had dumpsters out back, he could learn a lot from that. He might expect to find drug packaging materials like discarded stretch wrap rolls and vacuum-sealed containers sterilized with bleach. Parts of broken or old scales. Possibly, odor control items like petroleum jelly and motor oil. Items that would seem innocuous in the trash, but a trained eye would know their purpose.

These were some of the tricks Micah had learned back in his cartel days. How to package and sell drugs and get away with it. Not exactly resumé-building skills, but the knowledge did come in handy from time to time. Luis Velasquez's Sinaloa cartel had taught Michael McBriar many lessons, most of which, Micah wished he could now forget.

He met the corner of the building, still confident he'd been clear of the cameras. But when he turned the corner, it didn't matter what the cameras had seen.

He came face to face with the European gangster, leaning against the back of the building, smoking a clove cigarette. His hands were bloodied.

"What the hell?" the guy said. Definitely European, but Micah couldn't place the accent. He'd always been terrible at European geography. That feeling of familiarity intensified, but Micah still couldn't match a name to that face.

"Who the hell are you?"

"Templeton," Micah said. "Roland Templeton. I think I might have the wrong hangar. I'm supposed to meet a buddy of mine by the dumpsters."

"We do not have dumpsters."

Micah's eyes flitted to the man's bloodied hands, and the European noticed this. He dropped his cigarette and gritted his teeth, telegraphing a punch.

His left arm reared back, and Micah was already leaning to his right to dodge the blow. As the man's fist sailed past his face and he felt the whiff of air, he had a momentary pang of realization that he missed being in the boxing gym. Missed a lot of things he used to do, back when he was someone else.

No time to think about that now.

Micah jabbed the man in the gut, which made him lean forward, exposing his chin. Micah swept his other fist straight up, catching the guy underneath his jawbone. Micah made sure he extended the knuckle of his middle finger to give his punch the extra sting.

Even though the punch knocked the man's head back, he was only out of sorts for a split second. He lurched forward and stepped on Micah's foot, driving his heel down into Micah's toe.

Micah had been expecting a punch, and this move caught him completely off guard. With his foot pinned, he couldn't pull out of range of the guy's fists. The European took advantage and popped Micah cleanly on the cheek. Micah's teeth involuntarily gritted. He might have chomped his own tongue off if he hadn't anticipated the punch a split second before it had landed.

That would give him a black eye, no doubt about it.

Micah jabbed his thumbs into the guy's armpits to push him back and create a little space, but the European was sturdy. He barely moved an inch. Micah slid a step to the right and tried to drive his heel at the guy's knee, but his opponent swept his leg back and out of the way.

Now off balance, Micah couldn't steady himself when the guy pushed him, which sent Micah crumpling to the ground. A jolt of unease panicked Micah. This European was more skilled, more vicious, more agile. Micah thought himself clever in a fight, but this guy had him outmatched at every level.

The European was on him in a flash. He lunged forward and Micah barely had time to roll out of the way before the European landed on the ground. Micah threw his elbow at the man's exposed back, driving it with all his force.

Time to play dirty.

This blow knocked the air out of the European, and

before he could recover, Micah flung his other hand, palm open, at the back of the man's head. He slapped him hard enough to drive his face into the ground. That wet smack of flesh on concrete almost made him gag, but Micah couldn't waste the precious second of distraction.

He readied his hand to smack the guy again, but the back door started to open. He panicked. It could be Nathan, or Alec, or both of them. Maybe with guns.

He scrambled to his feet as the European was busy spitting blood on the concrete. Took one last peek, but still couldn't remember where he'd seen him before.

Micah dashed back around the corner as the door opened all the way. Didn't bother to check who had actually appeared through that open door.

He had to pray they hadn't seen his face. If he'd used up his anonymity, that would make everything much harder.

As he ran, he didn't bother to look back. But he was sprinting so wildly that his cap came flying off his head.

He'd have to abandon it, at first thinking it wasn't a big deal. If they were behind him and he turned, he'd be spotted. Not worth it.

But, as he neared the edge of the parking lot and met the street, he remembered who these guys supposedly had as friends. Cops. They had access to DNA testing. All it would take would be one swab of sweat off the inner brim of that hat, and they could find out the name Micah Reed.

Going back for the hat was not an option.

Micah sprinted across the street, barely managing not to be flattened by an oncoming truck. As he met the other side, he dared a glance back, and he saw Nathan or Alec

Auerbach stopping to pick up his baseball cap, halfway across the parking lot.

Shit.

Micah kept on running until he'd rounded the gas station, car keys in hand. Panting, dizzy, wanting only to reach the car as quickly as possible.

Maybe they wouldn't bother to test the hat for DNA.

Or maybe they would.

How long would it take to get those results back? Weeks? Days? Whatever it was, Micah was now on the clock.

# PART II

## HOW TO WIN FRIENDS AND INFLUENCE PEOPLE

~

## INSIDE WITSEC BLOG
## POST DATED 10.15

*Witness Protection began with the idea that if the government couldn't get imprisoned mobsters to testify against their own because of fear of revenge, then they'd never take down the mob. Some of those initial entrants were good people. Maybe they were accountants for the mob who'd never pulled a trigger. Or, they could have been honest businessmen in the community who were pressured by the mob to do things against their will. Maybe they had wives and children who'd be killed if they testified.*

*So, for those people, it makes sense to give them protection. To let them start over somewhere else.*

*But I read an article that said 95% of the entrants into WitSec are criminals themselves. Let that sink in for a moment. 95% of them are criminals. And these are the people we're wasting our taxpayer money on.*

*Your tax dollars, which you worked hard for and the government took from you, are going to buy houses and cars for people who have murdered other Americans. Stolen from them. And those houses might be in your neighborhood. Those cars might be driving on the streets next to where your children play.*

*You have no way to protect yourself from this, because there's no way for you to even know if this is happening right under your nose. Am I suggesting that you should fear everyone and everything around you? Not at all. That's not what it means* to be an American. But I feel like I have a right to know, and so do you.

If I move into a new house, I can look online to find out if there are any child molesters within five miles of me. But I can't look at some website to find out if the person living in the house next to me might have chopped up bodies with an axe, or sold drugs for a Mexican cartel, or kidnapped someone's child so he could get a payday.

If you knew that, would you stay there, or would you move?

This monster in your neighborhood gets a lifetime pass because he did one good thing in his miserable life. He testified. And that one good thing entitles him to walk around as a free man, no matter what heinous crimes he has committed in the past.

Stay tuned to the blog. I'm about to start naming names, and some of these are going to shock you.

∾

# CHAPTER NINE

**F**RANK WAITED. AND waited. For hours, he sat on the edge of the bed at the Baymont Inn, third floor, Tomás Zaluski's room. His old police baton across his knees. At first, he stayed on the bed closest to the door, across from the mirror. After he had grown tired of staring at himself in the mirror, he slid over to the other bed and rubbernecked at an art print of a medieval doctor wearing one of those long, beak-like masks. So bizarre, those things were. And what kind of hotel would have such a freaky picture on the wall?

Frank shook his head. Mountain towns.

Hours passed with no sign of Zaluski. Frank tried not to check his watch often, because time didn't seem to move. He'd be sure it had been at least an hour, then he'd tilt his wrist, and only fifteen minutes had elapsed. The agony of expectation.

He put some strong consideration into giving up. For

all he knew, Zaluski had seen him enter the inn, or some bellhop had tipped him off that an old black man was stalking the halls, asking about him. Frank didn't like to think his skills were slipping, but he was on the wrong side of sixty. Happened to everyone, eventually.

He stood, listening to his knees pop and crackle as he rose to his feet. Tired legs crossed the room, then he stared out the window at the blue rippling water of Lake Dillon, at the peaks of the mountains surrounding this cluster of little towns in the valley.

Spending more time in this room seemed like a waste.

With a sigh, he slipped the baton back into his bag and hoisted the bag over his shoulder. Hated giving up. Hated the prospect of losing the reward money, but odds were good that Zaluski was in the wind. That no amount of waiting was going to make the European magically appear and extend his wrists for the handcuffs.

Frank caught himself in the mirror again as he shuffled across the room. He hated the look of disappointment he read on his own reflection.

"Damn it, Frank, you came all this way. Now you're going to pack up and drive back to Denver with your tail between your legs?"

Maybe Frank didn't need to give up so easily.

What if Zaluski was still in town, and he had multiple rooms reserved in various hotels and motels? Maybe he was trying to throw Frank off by leaving this room to function only as a decoy. That seemed like a reasonable paranoid thing to do.

Frank crept back to the window and spied the parking lot. No one sitting in cars with eyes on this room. No one standing suspiciously, reading a newspaper, or staring at a phone. If Zaluski had aid, it wasn't nearby.

Frank left the room and eased into the hall, checking both ways for heads poking out of doors. Didn't look as if anyone had eyes on him. Then he saw the maid he'd paid for information exiting a room and crossing the hall to another. They made eye contact, and she winked at him. For all he knew, she'd sold him out to Zaluski herself.

He slipped down the hall to the back exit and ran down the stairwell. He paused at each floor's landing and gazed down the hall, trying to spot anything out of the ordinary. Nothing stood out.

Outside the building, Frank moseyed down Lusher Court to his car, gravel crunching under his feet. Despite the wonder and grandeur of the mountains surrounding these high-elevation towns, the towns themselves were usually little more than dirt and gravel. Not as much vegetation grew up here, so the street-level view wasn't quite so attractive.

Plus, being three thousand feet higher than Denver still could suck the wind out of him at an alarming rate. He'd tolerated the altitude better when he was younger, but he was getting too old for this, too. A tingling hand cinched his coat close around his body as a breeze rustled the trees.

He drove Summit Boulevard to Main Street, the only spot in town with a dense cluster of businesses and restaurants. If Zaluski could be found hanging out somewhere, he'd be there. Besides, Frank would do better at spotting him before the sun set. That was another change from his younger days. No one had ever explained to him that night vision was a luxury of youth.

Frank's stomach grumbled, and he could do a lot worse than an omelet and cinnamon roll from the Butterhorn Cafe. Breakfast for dinner never went out of style. He pulled a scarf from his trunk so he could wrap it around the lower half of his face. Zaluski didn't know Frank's face, but Frank had the advantage of anonymity, and he wanted to hold onto that as long as possible.

The tourist season was in its infancy, but plenty of people wandered along Main Street, from restaurants and shops. A lot of overpriced art galleries and driftwood sculpture-type places. Not Frank's style. Many of the signs featured the word *LOCAL* in giant block letters. As if the art was better if done by a mountain hippie versus some hippie from Chicago or New York.

With the baton inside his jacket, he strolled toward the Butterhorn, letting his eyes scan in all directions. Trying to watch out for a glimpse of Zaluski. Frank had no proof, but he kept a tight grip on the feeling that the bail jumper could still be here, somewhere. The old cop hunch had worked out so well for him so many times in the past.

Outside the Butterhorn, Frank paused and looked in through the window. Inside, he saw two plainclothes cops seated, digging forks and knives into plates of biscuits and gravy. Their backs were to him, but Frank saw the bottom of a gold badge clipped to one of their belts when the guy reached for the salt.

In Denver, a gold badge usually meant detective. Summit County PD had all silver badges. So these weren't Frisco cops, these were *Denver* cops.

Frank knew exactly why they were here.

He had competition.

## CHAPTER TEN

**D**AISY SAT OUTSIDE Nathan's house in Broomfield, thinking she was probably the most stupid person alive. Her hands circled the steering wheel, and she kept staring at the windshield, noting the dried streaks of washer fluid.

*Come over for breakfast,* he'd said. *We need to talk.*

She should be on a plane to Las Cruces now, and she would be, were it not for the roots she'd put down here in Colorado. The prison she'd made for herself in this cold and snowy place.

Also, that she wouldn't be able to afford a plane ticket to New Mexico. Not without Nathan's money.

Maybe she should have ignored his texts. Maybe she should have gone to stay with a friend, as she'd thought she could do before. Before Nathan had seen her suitcase leaning against the front door.

It was probably no longer an option.

And now, here she was, about to walk into his lavish house to have breakfast with him. So, so stupid.

She wiped tears from her cheeks and checked her makeup in the mirror before stepping out of the car. The breezy morning air sent her hair flying into her face and she stumbled.

Nathan opened the door, smiling at her. Daisy wanted to believe the smile was genuine. But since seeing him counting money with his buddies, he hadn't been the same. He'd looked at her with suspicious eyes.

He lifted a hand to wave and she crossed his front yard to meet him. She'd have to hug him, but she didn't want to. Daisy closed her eyes as he wrapped his arms around her. He was speaking, but the words were a warble lost in the slipstream.

He held her out at arm's length. "You okay?"

She nodded, smiling vigorously.

"What time does your shift start?" he said.

"Eleven."

"Excellent. Plenty of time for breakfast."

He stepped back inside his doorway and ushered her in. She crossed the threshold into the mansion, now seeing the marble and sparkling chandeliers differently. She'd always assumed that he'd come from money, had inherited enough to pay for this house and buy her condo, but maybe not.

*Drugs,* Micah had said. *It's always drugs.*

He walked into the kitchen, and for a split second, she considered not following him. Considered fleeing. A stronger person wouldn't have even come today, but she didn't know how to straddle this line of faking a relationship while simultaneously investigating what he was up to.

"I'll be right back," she said as she scurried up the stairs to the bathroom. Once inside the comfort of the four enclosed walls, she slumped on the toilet and pulled on the roll of toilet paper until she had enough for two handfuls. She bunched them in her palms, squeezing. The pressure against her hands felt reassuring, for some reason.

Part of her wanted to believe Nathan was a good man. That he had a perfectly valid explanation for what had happened the other day. And part of her knew she was foolish to think that. Nathan always had his dark side, his private side. He kept secrets, but Daisy never pried into his business. She'd sometimes assumed an affair, and if she asked too many questions, he would get angry.

Daisy didn't want to spur his anger. She'd seen how quickly he could morph from stillness to a thunderstorm. Like a firecracker popping, it came from nowhere and the suddenness always terrified her.

But, then why was she here? Why had she come to his house this morning?

"Babe?" he said from downstairs. "Breakfast is almost ready."

She dropped the wads of toilet paper in the trash and ran a hand through her hair. Maybe this was all in her mind. She'd been so confused lately, and maybe he had a perfect explanation.

When she left the bathroom and approached the top of the stairs, he was looming in the kitchen doorway below. He crossed his arms, frowning. She hurried down the stairs and followed him into the kitchen, where he left her to stir a pan of eggs on the stove.

"I have to go out of town for a couple days," he said. "I wanted to see you before I left. I know how much you hate your inconsistent schedule at the coffee shop, but seems like it works out well, for once."

"Oh," she said, trying to sound engaged, but not suspicious. A month or two ago, she would have asked him where he was going, but now she didn't want to know. Didn't want to watch him evade the question or invent some outright lie.

With narrowed eyes, he wiped his hands on a dishrag and folded his arms across his chest. "I need to ask you something, and it's serious."

Her heart leaped into her throat. She couldn't answer him.

"Two days ago, at your condo. You had a suitcase in the living room."

"Yes?"

"What was that about? Were you planning a trip I didn't know about?"

She sputtered, trying to invent something reasonable. "Exterminator. I was going to have him come, and I was going to stay at a motel for the night."

"Oh? Did you?"

"No, he canceled."

He frowned. Wasn't buying it. "Did you think about how those chemicals might affect Caden? You need to research those kinds of things."

She wished he wouldn't say Caden's name out loud. Coming from Nathan's lips, it felt like a threat.

"You're right," she said. "I should have done that."

He resumed stirring the eggs.

"Is that what you wanted to talk to me about?" she said. "Is the exterminator something I should let you arrange?"

He didn't answer at first, only turned off the heat and ladled the eggs onto two plates, each with sausage and steaming potatoes. He carried the plates to the table, set them down, and pointed at a chair.

Daisy sat.

Nathan took his seat and forked some eggs into his mouth. "I don't care about the exterminator. You can set that up however you want."

"Oh."

"No, I wanted to talk to you about something else. Sunday night, you showed up here unannounced."

She picked up her knife and fork. The knife was serrated, but not sharp. She couldn't defend herself with it. "You already apologized for that. We don't need to talk about it anymore. I understand I should ask before coming over."

"I'm not going to apologize. That's not what we need to talk about. I want to know what you think was happening here the other night."

"What do you mean?"

He set down his fork and sighed. "Come on, Daisy. I know you're different these last few days. I mean, look at you. You're trembling."

"I'm having one of those days. Having some cravings today."

He slammed his fist on the table, making the plates and silverware rattle. "Goddamn it, stop lying to me. You can say anything you want, but don't lie to me."

The trembling turned into a shake as tears rolled down her cheeks. "I don't know what I saw. And if I did see anything, I won't talk about it to anybody. I don't care what you were doing and it's none of my business."

This answer didn't satisfy him. Nathan snatched his plate and flung it over her head. She ducked and screamed as it crashed against the wall, splintering into pieces. Bits of plate clattered to the floor.

He jumped up and rounded the table in a flash. Before she could do anything to stop it, he was on her. Grabbed her by the wrists.

"Please, Nathan, I won't say anything."

"Not good enough," he said, growling.

# CHAPTER ELEVEN

MICAH LEANED CLOSE to the mirror, poking at the bluish tint under his eye. It hurt when he touched it, so he didn't know why he kept doing it. He hadn't been punched in the face for so long, he'd almost forgotten what it felt like.

Not great. But a punch was better than a knife wound or a bullet hole.

"Chicks dig scars," he said to Boba Fett's severed head, sitting in the soap tray, "but how do they feel about black eyes? Less sexy, or more sexy?"

Boba Fett said nothing.

Micah tried on his sunglasses, and they covered enough of the black eye that he could pass for normal, but that wouldn't help if he had to venture indoors. Unless he wanted to be the kind of person who wore sunglasses indoors, and he did not.

But what bothered him more than the black eye the vaguely-familiar European guy had given him was leaving his baseball cap behind at the hangar. It wasn't a remarkable thing, a light blue Denver Nuggets cap with the classic logo of the city outline and mountains. He considered himself more of an Oklahoma City Thunder fan since he'd grown up in the Sooner state. Not that he was a big basketball fan in general. The Nuggets cap helped him blend in a little better as a Denverite since he'd only lived in this adopted city for a couple years. He didn't like anyone linking him to Oklahoma if he could help it.

That link might cost him his life, if word got back to the people who were still offering a price on his head. None of those people had proof that Micah was still alive, of course. If they could have proved it, he and his family would already be dead.

Maybe that was pure paranoia. He'd told people in AA that he was from Oklahoma, although he lied about where he had attended High School and other specifics.

And whatever logo was stitched on the cap, it didn't matter now. It was in the hands of people who could possibly use it to find out who he was.

A fat thumb of doubt pressed down on Micah's head. He wasn't sure if pursuing this line of investigation into Nathan Auerbach and his people was worth it. Micah didn't have any reason to doubt what Daisy had said, but if her boyfriend was mixed up with the cops, that might be more trouble than it was worth.

Or if the cop angle was even true. Daisy had pointed Micah to a nameless cop who worked in Boulder, but no way would Micah take the thirty-minute drive to that little college town and put himself in danger.

Crooked cop or not, Micah didn't like interacting with the police, under any circumstances.

A knock came at the door.

Micah took off the sunglasses and snatched up Boba Fett, then crossed the living room to open the front door. There stood Daisy, tears streaming down her cheeks. A hooded sweatshirt shrouded her face.

She was wearing sunglasses, indoors.

"Can I come in?" she said.

He retreated a step, allowing her a path inside. She was hesitant, holding her purse out in front of her like a shield.

"What happened?" he said.

Daisy lowered the hood of her sweatshirt. Slipped off her sunglasses, and she was sporting an identical black eye. "I see you also had some trouble," she said, nodding at his eye. There was no humor in her words. Like a statement of fact.

"Forget about me. Tell me how this happened to you."

She averted her eyes, shook her head.

"It was him, wasn't it?"

Her tears flowed faster as she winced. "I tried to go stay with a friend, like you said, but he found out. He knows I saw him with the money the other night. He knows everything."

Micah took her hand and escorted her to the couch. He felt the pinch of guilt that it was his fault she'd been hurt, but he pushed it away. He hadn't done this. "Listen to me, Daisy. It's going to be okay. But I need to know a couple things, alright?"

She nodded, sniffling. Micah reached behind him to the end table and grabbed a box of tissues.

"Okay," she said.

"What about coming to see me at Frank's office? Did he say anything about that?"

She shrugged. "I don't think so."

"If he doesn't know about Frank and me, then we're okay. We still have the upper hand."

"If you say so. Everything feels like it's swirling around the toilet drain right now."

"Should you be here with me? Do you think he followed you?"

"Nathan said he was going out of town for a couple days. I saw him leave in his car."

Looking at her, so genuinely sad, Micah made a decision. He had to help this woman. Even if it involved mixing with cops who might or might not be crooked. Micah wasn't sure he believed that part of her story, but the details didn't matter right now.

"I'm going to fix this," he said, with a confidence he couldn't back up. But he had to say something. She was about to break down in front of him.

"Will you come to my apartment with me?" she said. "I have to get ready to leave for work soon, and I'm scared to go alone. I don't want a bodyguard, but it's just this one time."

He nodded and followed her out of the condo and to the elevator. Micah didn't know what to say to make her feel better. He was brimming with anger at this Nathan character, this expensive-car-driving asshole who thought it was okay to hit women.

Micah wanted to break his face, for that fact alone. Nathan deserved a lot more than a black eye in return.

Daisy paused outside her door, clutching the key. "It's messy."

"That's okay. Mine usually is too. You happened to visit me on a rare clean day."

She opened the door and he emerged into a mirror of his own condo. Different furniture, but the layout was the same. As he examined her living room, he noted a strange contraption in one corner. Like a mini-trampoline but enclosed with mesh on all four sides.

"What's that?" he said.

"Pack 'n Play."

Micah cocked his head, confused for a second. Then, he noticed the piles of toys on the floor around the Pack 'n Play. Stuffed animals, colorful little blocks, books with thick cardboard pages.

One framed picture on the wall of a baby wrapped in a blanket.

"You have kids."

She dropped her purse on the kitchen table and removed her sunglasses. "Just one."

She gripped her shoulder with a hand, digging her thumb into it. She winced as she massaged herself. Micah felt an urge to rush to her and massage her shoulders for her, but he had to resist. If he did that and she flinched from his touch, he'd feel awful.

She looked at him and he studied her, now seeing a bruise on her neck, too. What had Nathan done to her?

"Caden is sixteen months," she said.

He didn't hear or see any little humans running around. "Where is the little guy?"

Her lip trembled. "He's with his dad."

"That's not... is he with Nathan?"

"No, no, not him. Me and Caden's dad split up a long time ago." Her tears resumed, and she tried to speak, but what came out next sounded garbled. "I lost... I had some problems. They took him away. I get to see him sometimes, but they don't... I don't have custody."

Micah's curiosity burned at him to ask what kind of problems, but he kept his mouth shut. She disappeared into the kitchen and took a pitcher of tea from the fridge. She lifted it at him, and he nodded. Wasn't much of a tea drinker, but he wasn't going to turn her down.

She poured him a glass, quietly sniffling and biting back her tears. As he lifted the drink to his mouth, he had that split second fear that it might have alcohol in it. You never know what some people might think is fun. He didn't think Daisy would spike his tea, but he sniffed to be sure. Even after a year sober, he still knew he couldn't take even a single drink.

"I've been doing better," she said. "Going to my meetings. That's the only reason I get to see Caden at all."

"Meetings?"

"The Narcotics Anonymous meetings," she said.

Although Micah was an alcoholic, he'd had his share of

the other stuff, too. He dug into his pocket and retrieved his one year AA chip. Held it out to her.

"You're sober?" she said. Seemed genuinely surprised.

He nodded. "How long do you have?"

"Sixty-four days."

"That's a rough spot. It does get better, though."

"A whole year," she said, taking the chip from his hand. She rubbed her thumb back and forth across it. "What's it like to have a year?"

"I'm not holding on for dear life anymore, but like you, I'm only one drink or drug away from slipping back into it all."

She returned his chip. "This morning, my sponsor told me she thinks I'm a chameleon, but I don't know what that means."

"That you're adaptable? Or you can hide in plain sight?"

She paused, sniffling. "Maybe. I know I need to stay clean and work the steps if I want to be a part of my son's life. And I want that more than anything. Caden is all I think about when he's not here."

Micah had no kids that he knew of, so he had no idea about the longing she was experiencing. But he knew how it felt to be early in sobriety. He and Daisy had more in common than he'd first realized.

"I'm trying, though," she said, "to do the things I love. I'm going to play at the Bardo on Speer tomorrow night. It'll be my first gig since giving up the cocaine."

"You play what? guitar?"

She nodded. "I also try to sing." She managed a little smile. "Not very well, though."

"I play guitar, too."

She smiled, a genuine upturning of the corners of her lips. "You should come see me play. Maybe you can give me some pointers."

## CHAPTER TWELVE

MICAH SPENT PART of the morning at home, trying to verify Daisy's assertion that Nathan had left town. Micah kept coming up empty.

Nathan didn't leave much of a paper trail. That domestic abuser seemed to be squeaky clean, in every way that counted. He didn't have traceable offshore bank accounts, no criminal record, and no strange business partnerships with shady European front companies.

His twin brother Alec was equally a mystery. He worked in medical device sales, specifically for a company that manufactured sonogram equipment. Pretty boring stuff. But, given the car Micah had seen Alec driving the other day, he was either the best damn sonogram machine salesman ever or he was in the same shady business as his brother.

Whatever business that was.

Micah wanted more information before returning to

the private hangar at the airport to attempt another break-in. That hangar was owned by a company named Twin Engine LLC, which seemed like some shell that existed in name only. Micah couldn't track them through tax documents, through public filings, or anything.

These Auerbach brothers were meticulous and invisible. They had no literal connection to Twin Engine LLC, but the name connection seemed obvious. How had they hidden it so well?

He kept hitting dead ends, so he decided to take part of the morning off and distract himself for a while. His old habit of popping off a few rounds at the shooting range didn't seem appealing right now, but he knew of another place in the same neighborhood that might help him get his fix.

After hitting a morning AA meeting, he drove into the Five Points neighborhood of Denver, past the gun range he used to frequent. He cruised by the Pink Door, the strip club where he'd spent the night of his last drink, over a year ago. His memories of that night were vague and splotchy. And it was fine with him if they stayed that way. Some demons were better left to be seen through a blurry lens.

Past the Pink Door, he pulled into the parking lot at Glazer's gym. A run-down, dirty place with shabby outsides and insides. Exactly what Micah was looking for. He didn't want some fancy gym with an organic smart juice bar and personal trainers in polo shirts. No, sometimes you crave a grungy and smelly dive to throw some punches at a beat up bag held together with duct tape.

When Micah opened the front door, that stink of sweat was unmistakeable. Like coming home, he used to box at a place like this in Oklahoma City with his best friend. And never once since his friend had died.

He purchased a six-month membership to the gym with no hassle, and that was another thing he appreciated. No testosterone-riddled high-pressure sales people. The grumbly sales guy couldn't have cared less whether Micah joined or not.

After a quick change and a few stretches, he went to work on a heavy bag. With each punch he threw, he imagined Nathan's face crumpling under his knuckles. The kind of man who would ever hit a woman deserved to be pummeled, and Micah could only hope he would get the chance someday.

"You are playing with fire, asshole," said a voice behind him.

Micah halted, panting, and turned to find two men facing off. They were about twenty feet away, standing between the two main boxing rings. The men were pointing fingers in each other's chests, shoulders high and stances wide, like cons in the yard. No one backing down.

"You're going to threaten me?" One of the guys said. "I will kill your ass."

Just then, a beefy man with buzzcut blond hair appeared next to the two men. Muscle shirt, tattoos, square jaw. He was holding a bucket in one hand, a flex grip in the other, towel slung over his shoulder. Madly pumping away at the flex grip.

"Guys," the beefy one said as he shoved the flex grip in

his pocket. "Settle down, or take it outside. Or put on pads and get in the ring. Don't be children."

One of the two arguers tossed a punch, and the beefy peacemaker threw up a hand to block it, then he wrapped his hand around the guy's wrist. With a quick tug, he pulled that wrist away from the guy's body and jerked it downward, which drove him to his knees.

Micah's eyes shot wide open. This beefy guy was light-ning-quick. The towel didn't even slip from its spot over his shoulder as he restrained one of the two combatants. The other guy took a step back, hands up, head shaking.

"Not inside the gym," Beefy Guy said. "I already told you once. Now both of you, get the hell out of here."

The two guys backed off, the one who'd thrown the punch rubbed his shoulder socket, wincing. Not so tough now that he'd had his ass handed to him with half the gym watching.

Beefy guy picked up his bucket and strode off, which placed him directly in Micah's path.

"Hey," Micah said as the guy neared him.

"What's up, man?"

"Do you work here?"

The guy looked down at the bucket in his hand and grinned. "Actually, I don't. I know the owner, though, so I'm helping out for the day. They're short-handed and I'm doing the guy a favor."

"Oh," Micah said. "I was going to ask you for some pointers on this heavy bag. Been a while."

The guy put down his bucket and extended a hand. "Layne Parrish. I'd be happy to help."

Micah shook, and he had to flex his arm to meet the force of Layne's grip. Told the guy his name. He didn't like to do that if he could help it, but Layne's combination of brawn and his childish grin was somehow endearing to Micah. He got the *blink test* feeling that this guy was okay.

Layne waved his hand at the bag, and Micah tossed a few punches at it. Layne watched intently. Made little grunting noises as he bobbed his head.

"Not bad, man," Layne said. "Seriously, you got some style and you're quick as a whip. But with the heavy bag, you're looking for power, not finesse. It's more about the hips that you might think. You're pushing from your shoulders. Wastes a lot of energy that way."

Layne squared off with the bag, sneered, and pounded it a few times. Micah tried to keep his eyes from bulging out of their sockets. The poor bag threatened to fly apart with each wallop it took. Layne's teeth gritted with a fury in every punch, and he pushed out his breaths like grunts between each movement. His biceps seemed to grow to twice their size.

Layne stepped back and waved to the bag, and Micah gave it a few goes, throwing his hips into it. Layne had been right. His punches landed harder, he recovered faster, and he felt less pull on his muscles.

"There you go, man," Layne said, rubbing the towel on the back of his neck.

"You were totally right about the hips."

Layne pointed at an unused boxing ring in the corner. "Want to spar a little?"

"With you? Are you crazy?"

Layne chuckled. "Maybe I can show you how to protect yourself from black eyes." He pointed at Micah's shiner and Micah involuntarily turned his head. He'd stopped thinking about it since he'd left his condo this morning.

"Thanks, but I'll pass," Micah said.

Layne shrugged and wandered off, and Micah returned to working the bag. He hardly ever made small talk with people. Even a few months ago, Micah would have felt so unsure—in the early days of his sobriety—that talking with strangers would have filled his stomach with rabid butterflies. But Layne didn't freak him out at all, and that fact was freaky in itself. Micah usually operated from a place of paranoia as a baseline. He hated being that way, but the practice of it had kept him alive for the few years since the trial and Witness Protection.

After thirty minutes of bag work and some light cardio, Micah hit the showers and left the gym. When he opened the door, Layne was in the parking lot, fiddling with the engine of a black Harley Davidson motorcycle.

As Micah was considering raising his collar and walking in an arc around him, Layne lifted his head. Gave him a wave.

Shit. Micah didn't have much choice other than to approach Layne to say hi. This would mean more small talk, and now Micah did feel a twinge of anxiety in his stomach. One conversation was happenstance. Two meant he was getting to know a person.

"How was your workout?" Layne said as Micah came within spitting distance.

"Good. I'm exhausted. I've been lazy lately and it feels good to be tired like this again."

"I hear you, man," Layne said. "I'm on the road so much, I don't get to hit the gym as much as I'd like."

"What do you do?"

"Well, I'm retired, but I do some security consulting on the side."

Micah thought Layne appeared a little young to be retired. He couldn't have been more than four or five years older than Micah. Maybe thirty-five, tops. And Layne didn't look like the retired-at-twenty-five Silicon Valley entrepreneur type.

Layne must have noticed Micah's raised eyebrow, because he added, "army."

Micah now surveyed one of the tattoos on Layne's shoulder. A skull wearing a beret, with the word *Ranger* behind it. It was faded and slightly stretched.

Layne opened a bag slung over the back of the Harley and removed two silver cans. Micah shied away at first.

Layne jerked his hands back, looking confused. "Did I scare you?"

Then, Micah realized they weren't beer cans, but protein drinks. "No, I just... I thought those were beers. I don't drink."

"Oh, I gotcha. I rarely do. It's hell on your body when you're trying to train, so I usually stay away from the stuff."

Micah accepted the protein drink and sipped at it, and he kept getting the feeling that this Layne guy had no hidden agenda. And that observation unnerved him because he didn't usually get that sense from people. Or, if he did, he tried his hardest to ignore it.

So they drank their chocolate protein shakes and chatted about the weather, about the Broncos' chances this season, and about a lot of nonsense. By the end of their conversation, they'd exchanged phone numbers and agreed to meet back at the gym in a couple days. Layne promised he'd go easy on him in the ring, but Micah wasn't so sure about that.

~

INSIDE WITSEC BLOG
POST DATED 10.16

*Jermaine Orlovsky was part of the US Marshal's service for more than twenty years. Like a lot of the other people who worked with WitSec, he didn't like the idea of associating with criminals at first. Didn't like coddling bad people (I can relate).*

*But he came to like his job, and he was good at it. Had spotless performance reviews every quarter, and he always got the full merit increase every year.*

*He came to feel that he was doing "good things" for people by making sure the entrants to WitSec were cared for.*

*You could say that Jermaine became dedicated.*

*At the tail end of a long and decorated career, Jermaine was tasked with protecting Sonny Catalino, a gangster from Philadelphia. Sonny was a real bad guy, in every sense of the word. He'd killed people, or at least the government had suspected him of killing people. Nothing could ever stick. When they eventually did catch him, it was for trying to pass counterfeit bills. Can you believe that? Such a stupid thing to get caught for.*

*Anyway, Sonny decided to rat on his mob buddies, rather than go to prison for twenty years. In exchange for testifying, he served six months on a lesser charge. When he got out, he joined WitSec, and Jermaine became his handler. Helped him move from Philly to Seattle, where Sonny was supposedly working as a loan officer at a bank.*

*The thing is, he wasn't. Sonny figured out how to embezzle (thank God for spellcheck, because I would have never figured out how to spell that word on my own) money from the bank. And what's even crazier is that he enlisted Jermaine's help to do it. A criminal and a cop, working side by side to steal money from regular people in Seattle.*

*Of course, they got caught. When the sting went down, local cops had no idea who they were arresting (since WitSec is so hush hush) and both Sonny's and Jermaine's faces ended up on television. This was a big bust for Seattle PD, the kind that ends with everyone getting promoted.*

*Not Sonny and Jermaine, though. They were both dead within a week. The mob doesn't take kindly to snitches, and all it took was one news story for Sonny's old employers to find him. And Jermaine had to die too, because that's how the mob is.*

*So the moral of this story is, maybe you think you're a good guy, working for the government, helping people. But if you lie down with dogs, you're going to get up with fleas.*

*Starting in the next post, I'm going to give you names. Names of people who had been arrested, and are now living new lives with new names. Don't miss the next post.*

≈

# CHAPTER THIRTEEN

M ICAH SAT ON his couch, staring at his phone, reading the latest post from the Inside WitSec blog. The next post would name people in the WitSec program. If only the author of this blog had any idea of the collateral damage his actions were going to cause. The parents, the siblings, the children who would be destroyed by having these former criminals outed.

But Micah couldn't do anything about it. He could only watch from the sidelines, reading these posts as they appeared on the internet.

He abandoned the couch, grabbed a coat, and unearthed his battered Honda Accord from the parking garage to head back out toward the airport. Today, he was going to take another crack at getting access to that private hangar. Another attempt to find out what the hell was going on inside there, and what Nathan might be doing.

He flashed back on the beefy Army Ranger Layne Parrish from this morning, and how he'd said he worked in *security consulting*. Micah wasn't quite clear what that meant, but if it had something to do with security systems, Layne's skills could prove useful in a situation like this.

But no way would Micah call up this virtual stranger and ask him to help break into a building by the airport. He'd only met the guy today. For all he knew, Layne would call the cops on him.

Micah again parked behind the nearby gas station, intending to cross the street and walk to the hangar. But as he was about to leave his car, a lanky and impossibly thin woman stumbled around the back of the gas station. She looked drunk, barely able to keep herself upright. Her eyes were on the bathrooms at the rear of the building, but her feet swayed and she couldn't walk in a straight line. She tripped over herself and her purse fell from her shoulder, onto the ground. When she bent to pick it up, she lurched and vomited everywhere. On the side of the building, on her shoes, into her purse.

Micah winced. He'd done this kind of thing back in his drinking career, more than once. Been thrown out of bars, wandered home, drenched in his own vomit. Woken up covered in stink, consumed by shame until the new day's alcohol binge helped him forget how much he hated himself.

Micah hoped he wouldn't ever have to feel that way again. Never wanted to be that person drowning in shame. And he wouldn't have to, as long as he stayed sober.

He was about to leave his car and offer the lady some

help when she slung her vomit-stained purse over her shoulder and lumbered to the other side of the building. A minute later, she left in the passenger seat of some guy's truck. At least she wasn't driving.

Now alone, Micah headed for the hangar. As he had last time, he kept his movements in a wide arc, making it look as if he was going to walk past it. No cars out front. No sounds emanating from the hangar, no indication of any light or motion on the inside. The only windows were up high enough that he couldn't see through them.

He checked the parking lot for the baseball cap he'd dropped, but it wasn't there. That would have been a lucky break of the type Micah never seemed to land.

This time on his approach, Micah didn't make the mistake of blindly turning around to the back of the building. He walked far past it, avoiding potential surprise meetings with sketchy European gangsters. After completing a circle of the hangar and finding no sign that anyone was inside or outside the building, he made his approach. He skulked straight for that back door where he'd encountered the gangster the other day. It was a reinforced steel door with keycard entry and no physical lock. Micah's lock picking skills didn't extend to digital.

"Shit, Boba," Micah said as he thumbed the nub of Boba Fett's head through his jeans, "we can't do anything with this."

He sat against the metal exterior of the building and breathed for a few seconds. From the main airport, a plane took off, sending vibrations through the hangar and making Micah's nose tingle.

Maybe if he had a blowtorch, he could cut a hole in the side of the building. But that wouldn't exactly be *Leave No Trace* kind of stealth.

In the movies, high-tech spies would spray something on the keypad and use a cutting-edge ultraviolet thingy to get a heat map and figure out the key combination. But that was the movies.

He toyed with the idea of breaking into Nathan's house, but something told him the Auerbach brothers wouldn't leave their keycards sitting around. If he knew who that European gangster was, or if he knew how to find Nathan or Alec Auerbach, he could try to pickpocket it from them, but he didn't know where any of those three were.

Dead ends, everywhere.

Micah rounded the building again, looking for anything with a lock or some way he might be able to gain access through a grate. No dice anywhere he looked.

He circled the edge of the property, looking for a drain that led out, or something he could use to bypass the doors. Maybe even a way to get up to the roof of this giant building to break into a skylight or something. But he kept coming up empty.

If he stayed out here, surveying this building much longer, someone was going to see him acting suspiciously and call the cops. Micah wasn't getting into that building easily, not unless he had some help.

# CHAPTER FOURTEEN

YESTERDAY, FRANK HAD spotted Zaluski's Lamborghini cruising along Main Street in Frisco while he was out for a walk. The sleek car crawled along the street like a panther, shoulders poking out, ready to pounce. Frank assumed it was Zaluski's based on the color and the year, but he couldn't be one hundred percent sure. The windows were tinted to an almost-night shade of black.

Since Frank was on foot, he struggled to keep pace with the car as it drove down Main. Obviously, Frank didn't want to sprint after it, but after the car had turned onto a neighborhood side street, he broke out into a jog.

By the time Frank had caught up to the car, it appeared abandoned. Parked along some barren street with no sign of motion inside. Couldn't have been more than two minutes since it had turned on the side street. Frank immediately assumed Zaluski had been spooked, so he walked past, eyes averted, in case Zaluski was still inside.

Frank had no reason to think his target knew his face, but wasn't taking any chances.

After a few minutes, the car doors still had not opened. Even through the tint, Frank could see a little of the interior, and it looked empty. So he studied the nearby houses, peeking through windows, hoping to spot the bail jumper.

Zaluski didn't reveal himself, and Frank didn't want to overstay his welcome on this street, so he slipped a tiny GPS tracker from his pocket. He strolled by the car and attached the little magnetic gizmo to the top of the tailpipe.

He casually walked to Abbey's Coffee to get WiFi, opened his laptop, and synced with the tracker. Two hours elapsed with no movement from the car. Just a pulsing dot staying in the same spot. A couple times, Frank left the coffee shop and jogged down the street to check if the car was still there, and then hurried back to the coffee shop to resume surveillance.

After another hour with no movement, Frank left the coffee shop again, but this time, the car was gone, and the tracker was sitting in the snow next to the street.

"Son of a bitch," Frank said as he retrieved his tracker from the snow.

Zaluski hadn't returned to the Baymont Inn, either, and Frank knew that because he was staying in the room next door. No, that room had to be a decoy. The European was clever, that was for sure.

But Zaluski was still in Frisco. Frank was certain. There were Denver cops in town, looking for him.

But Frank was going to find him first.

What bothered Frank was that if Zaluski had jumped bail, why wouldn't he flee the country? Why would he stay in the same state where he was facing drug charges, giving himself the chance to be captured? It didn't make sense. There had to be something important going on that Zaluski would take such a risk.

Something bigger was going on here, but Frank didn't have enough info to connect it all together.

The next morning, he decided to take a walk down to Lake Dillon to clear his head. When he rounded the first corner on the lakeside trail, that's when he realized he was being followed. It began as hints of motion in his peripheral, then he noticed someone back there was matching his steps and turns around the lake.

He moseyed along the trail, dodging all the cyclists who sped by on their street bikes, whirring like hummingbirds. Lycra and spandex whipping past at warp speed.

The person following him was good. A professional. Frank couldn't spot more than a hint of a person anytime he angled his head to catch a glimpse.

But Frank was smarter. Maybe he didn't have the physical skills he'd had at twenty-five, but he had a lifetime of experience, and he knew how to blow a tail. In some places, the trail skirted a few feet away from the lake edge, diverting the path into clusters of trees. All Frank had to do was wait for a group of bikers to pass, then duck into those trees and double back.

But this tail, he didn't want to lose, he wanted to reverse the game.

So he took a quick turn after a thicket of trees and

slipped into the brush between the path and the lake. And he waited. Five minutes later came one of the detectives he'd seen at the Butterhorn Cafe. Heavy wool coat on over his suit.

Two days ago, he hadn't paid much attention to the two in the cafe, other than to ID them by their clothes and their Denver-style badges. But now, as this man in his aviator sunglasses strolled by, pretending to enjoy the view, Frank recognized him. And Frank was so surprised, he abandoned his hiding spot and rejoined the path. Here was his competition to nab Zaluski, now tailing him.

"Everett Welker," Frank said.

The detective spun, put his hands on his hips. He did an admirable job of pretending he wasn't disappointed that Frank had gotten the drop on him. "Frank Mueller. I'll be damned, you old bastard. Long time no see."

Everett approached Frank with a hand extended. Frank eyed the hand, considered not shaking it. Everett Welker was an ambitious cop that Frank had no trouble believing had made detective quickly. He'd been only a uniformed officer when Frank was already entertaining fantasies of his retirement. Ambitious, opportunistic, dreams of being the kind of cop who gets on the news, gets gigs to consult on Hollywood movies. He was also the kind of cop that, if Internal Affairs had ever come to Frank with questions about him, Frank wouldn't have been surprised one bit.

A few years had elapsed since they'd seen each other, but Everett looked the same. A little less hair on top, a few more wrinkles around his mouth, but he still wore that same smarmy grin.

Frank did shake his hand. "I thought Denver cops stayed out of the mountains."

"And I thought black guys didn't like the cold."

Ahh, right. Frank had almost banished this crucial detail to the Lost Memories section of his brain. Everett was a racist, too, and that was the other reason Frank couldn't stand him.

Everett returned his hands to his sides, then he brushed his coat back to expose the gun on his hip and the badge clipped to his belt.

Everett held his serious face for a second, then he chuckled. "I'm messing with you, Frank. Haven't seen you in so long, I gotta bust your balls a little, right? What are you doing up here in Frisco?"

"I'm retired now, so I'm kicking around the mountains before tourist season gets underway. That's why I'm here. Why are you here, Everett?"

For a second, Frank thought Everett wasn't going to answer the question. His lips swished around like he was evening out some lip balm. "Well, yeah, Frank, I'm just kicking around, too."

## CHAPTER FIFTEEN

S INCE NATHAN WAS out of town, his twin Alec
wasn't anywhere to be found, and the European
brawler was a mystery, Micah focused his attention on the other people Daisy allegedly had seen the night
of the money-counting: cops. She hadn't been able to
name any of them, only given a description of the one who
she claimed was a Boulder County officer. Chubby, light
brown hair, furry mustache.

He didn't know why, but accepting this last part of her
story had been a challenge. One thing Micah had never
found in his research on Nathan and Alec Auerbach was a
connection with any police officers. No social media, no
financial links. As much as Micah wanted to believe in
Daisy's version of the events, he'd always had a sliver of
doubt about that part.

So he needed a closer look at this Boulder cop.

Not that Micah had a good history with the police.
Going on an in-person mission wasn't the smartest thing

he could do with his time. But he was out of leads, so he had to try something. Stomp the ground and see what snakes come out of the holes.

He stood in his condo building's elevator, debating whether to press *G* for the garage to get his car, or *2* to visit Daisy before leaving. Part of him wanted to talk to her, to be convinced that putting himself in danger was worth it.

With a sigh, he opted for the garage. He didn't know what Daisy could tell him to make him feel assured. This whole investigation was strange and confusing, with too many strands that led nowhere. And Micah would see her later tonight, anyway, at her coffee shop gig. At least, by then he would know if she'd been correct about the police being involved.

He drove up to Boulder and navigated around the CU campus to The Hill. This part of Boulder was comprised of shabby yet overpriced student housing and endless rows of frat houses, sub shops, and janky bars.

He parked near the police station and stood beside his car for a moment. A gaggle of sorority girls strolled along the sidewalk as he crossed the street. One of them—the obviously bold one in the group—stuck two fingers in her mouth to give him a suggestive cat-call whistle. The other girls giggled, and Micah raised a bashful hand in acknowledgment. The bold one made some kissy faces and was about to say something when her friends dragged her away, around the corner at the end of the block.

It's not every day a group of nubile young coeds shouts

at you like construction workers do, but Micah wasn't in the right state of mind to feel flattered.

Instead, he endured a sting of panic as his hand reached out to grip the handle and open the glass door. He'd hated dealing with these people, even before his poor experience with his handler from WitSec. He'd been arrested and assaulted by police officers, singled out— sometimes fairly and sometimes unfairly. Too many of them got off on the power trip of authority.

But he needed to do this. To finally believe Daisy's story. Or, if Daisy had been wrong about the cops, then having the law on his side could be the best option to figuring out how Nathan had limitless money.

Micah took a breath and opened the door.

Inside, he was at first startled by how clean and modern the building was. But, of course, he remembered he was in Boulder, that bastion of tech startups and opulent hillside houses and decided it was entirely normal that the police department wouldn't be a decaying relic like most.

There were comfortable waiting chairs in the lobby and a clean counter. Curved television screens hanging on the walls, showing various news channels.

Behind the counter sat a bony woman who smiled at him as he entered. "Can I help you?"

The smile jarred him. Micah was used to treating law enforcement as adversaries. Everyone except for Frank, and he didn't count, because the old man was retired.

"I need to speak with a detective," Micah said.

The woman tilted her head down, peering at him over her glasses. "Regarding?"

He had to make a split-second decision. Report the domestic abuse Daisy had experienced at Nathan's hand, which probably wouldn't go anywhere if she refused to press charges? No, keeping Daisy's name out of it would be the wiser choice. On the other hand, he could report the possible cop corruption angle, which was impossible to prove.

Micah chose neither. He'd stick with the money.

"I believe a crime has taken place. Something that needs to be investigated."

The woman waved him forward and she poised her hands above the keyboard. "And your name, sir?"

He hesitated. The idea that they might enter his name in some database hadn't occurred to him. He could give a fake one, but what if she asked for his ID? Like an idiot, he'd left his wallet in his back pocket. Could they press charges if he falsified his name?

"Micah Reed," he said, and she typed it without breaking his gaze.

Damn, he felt like such a chump.

"Okay, Mr. Reed, can you give me details about this crime?"

"Thank you, but I'd rather talk to a detective."

She soured but nodded anyway. With a little sigh, she pressed a hidden button somewhere and the door next to her counter buzzed. "Step inside, and park yourself on the benches to the right. Someone will be along to speak with you shortly."

He thanked her and entered the door into the innards of the police station. This room was a little more like what he was accustomed to seeing. Uniformed cops walking around, their waists lined with attachments and gadgets like Batman's belt. Mugs of coffee gripped in eager hands. Desks with *in* and *out* trays, which seemed archaic since each desk had a laptop.

He slid onto the bench near the door and watched the activity for a moment. Seeing those uniforms sped his heart. He couldn't help but think back to the night in Stillwater, right before the feds had first contacted him. The cop harassing him, attacking him, his fingers around Micah's throat. Micah defending himself, which resulted in the cop's death.

And Micah thinking his life was over. In a way, he'd been right.

Among the cops sitting at desks and walking about the room, he didn't see anyone who matched the description Daisy had provided: chubby, light brown hair, furry mustache.

In another minute, a man wearing suspenders with a gun in an armpit holster approached Micah, a little pad of paper in his hand. "Afternoon, Mr. Reed. They said you want to talk to me."

"I want to report a crime."

The detective didn't sit on the bench with him or invite Micah to come back to some office. He stood there, scribbling on his pad. "Uh-huh. I'm gonna need you to be more specific."

Micah sneered at the detective's sarcasm. "There's a

woman who lives in my building. She saw someone counting a large amount of money, and I think it's drug related. A *large* amount of money. The man's name is Nathan Auerbach."

At the mention of Nathan's name, the detective's eyes shot up from the pad at Micah. They shared an awkward look. It lasted less than a half a second, and then the detective resumed his writing, but it was enough to spook Micah. Make his skin tingle.

"And the woman's name?"

"Her name isn't important. She's a friend of mine, that's all."

The detective stopped writing, then he slipped his little notepad into his shirt pocket. "Okay, Mr. Reed, wait here, please. I'll be back in a minute to gather some more details."

The detective left, and Micah got the sense this was all going to end badly. He looked back at the door he'd entered through, wondered if he would be able to open it from the inside. He decided that if someone came through it now, he would bolt from his seat and scurry out before it had a chance to close. He was less than ten feet away. He could make it.

But as much as he wanted to leave, he knew he had to stay and see this through. He'd lit the fuse, now he had to find out what color the explosion would be. Maybe that was insane, sitting in a police station, unarmed, around a couple dozen men with firearms attached to them like limbs.

A moment later, Micah glanced up to find the

suspenders-wearing detective whispering to a uniform cop, and they both turned their heads to watch Micah.

His hand explored around for the nub that Boba Fett's head made in his jeans. His heart raced. Had to will his legs to keep him on the bench, while his brain kept shouting *leave leave leave*.

And even though he hadn't seen the cop Daisy had described, Micah felt like he had enough information to convince himself that she had actually seen what she'd claimed. He didn't want to be here any longer.

The detective approached him. "Mr. Reed, I think we can help you. If you'll come with me."

"I've changed my mind. I made a mistake, and I'm going to go."

The detective bit his lower lip. "I understand, sir. Whatever you want."

Micah turned toward the door back to the lobby, but the detective whistled. "Mr. Reed, you can't get out that way. Please, follow me. I'll show you the way out."

Micah held his hands behind his back and flexed his wrists, readying himself to fight. The last thing in the world he wanted was to get into a brawl inside the Boulder police department, but this day seemed headed in that direction. The firecracker's fuse had grown shorter.

Suspenders walked down a long hall, and Micah couldn't help but notice the looks some of the cops shot at him. Could they smell a former criminal? Did he have that *look* about him? Maybe they saw the fading black eye and assumed he was a thug.

An exit sign hung above a door at the end of the hallway. Micah started to think maybe he wasn't going to have to punch his way out here. But he realized that if they were going to rough him up, they would naturally do it outside.

So he ventured toward the door, saying nothing to Suspenders, and readied himself for a fight as soon as he stepped outside. He opened it and walked into an alley. The back of a row of sandwich shops to his right, exit to the parking lot on his left. But no one throwing a bag over his head or jabbing a stun gun at his side.

"Micah Reed," said a voice behind him.

Micah spun to find a uniform cop, chubby, with a perfectly-groomed cop mustache. Like a furry slug sitting on this guy's upper lip.

The cop had been leaning against the building, and he took a step forward, within striking distance of Micah. He had a gun and a taser and handcuffs on his belt, but they were all nestled in their holsters. The cop's hands were empty.

"What?" Micah said.

"Nathan Auerbach. You were asking about him."

"Was I?"

The cop grinned. "Mr. Auerbach is one of the top financial supporters of *see-fop* in Colorado. Did you know that?"

For a second, Micah was completely baffled at what the hell a *see-fop* was. Then, he realized it must have been *CFOP*, the Colorado Fraternal Order of Police. Micah hadn't found any kind of charitable contributions like this in Nathan's public records.

"I did not know that. But I don't see what it has to do with me."

The cop stepped closer, opening his mouth in a sneer. The slug of a mustache curved up with the man's lips. "It means you need to mind your own damn business."

The cop was close enough that Micah could grab his choice of weapons off the guy's belt. He could whip out that taser, drive it into the guy's gut, and put him on the ground before he ever knew what hit him. But Micah stood firm, with his hands on his hips.

Still Micah didn't feel obligated to give this cop any respect. "That's not a nice thing to say."

"Go home, unless you and Daisy want to end up in the trunk of someone's car."

Micah hadn't said Daisy's name in the police station. But, since the guy knew it, that meant he had to have been one of the cops Daisy had seen with Nathan, counting the money.

Daisy had been right, and telling the truth. Micah had no doubts anymore.

Micah and the cop both stood silent for a moment. Chests pointed at each other like growling dogs.

Micah glanced down at the cop's badge and noted his number. 402. He waited to see if the cop was going to throw a punch, but he only stood there. Maybe he was waiting for Micah to make the first move so he could put him in handcuffs.

"Anything else you want to say?" Micah said.

The cop sucked through his teeth, then shook his head once to the left. Maintained that steely gaze.

Then, Micah stepped back, lifted his palms in a show of surrender, and rounded the front of the building. He craned his neck to see if the cop was going to follow him.

Mustache cop stayed behind, probably content with the assumption that he'd scared Micah straight. But Micah now had confirmation that not only was Daisy telling the truth about what she'd seen, but it went way deeper than some guy selling drugs.

And Micah could no longer turn back.

# CHAPTER SIXTEEN

A FTER LEAVING BOULDER, Micah got a phone call from Layne, the beefy guy he'd met at the boxing gym that morning. Layne invited him out for a cup of coffee because he said he wouldn't be able to meet him at the gym the day after tomorrow, as they'd planned.

Micah almost said no, but then he heard Frank's voice in his head from Monday. *You're a year sober now, it's time to make some friends. Interact with normal people.*

So Micah drove to a Starbucks in LoHi, the neighborhood west of downtown Denver, and sat alone at a table. Cappuccino in front of him. He had an awkward feeling that this encounter was something like a date, but he hadn't gotten the impression Layne was hitting on him before. There'd been no longing looks, no blushing, and no deliberate physical contact. Layne seemed more likely to punch Micah in the arm than suggestively brush up against him.

After Micah had been waiting for about fifteen minutes, the door opened and in walked Layne, in corduroy slacks and another white t-shirt. Motorcycle helmet in one hand, and under his other arm was an enormous stuffed bunny. The thing was at least three feet tall and bright pink.

Layne set his motorcycle helmet on the table and put the bunny in the chair across from Micah. "Sorry I'm late, man. Let me grab some coffee and I'll be right with you."

Micah stared at the bunny as Layne left him. A couple minutes later, Layne pulled a chair from a nearby table so he could sit. The bunny remained in its own chair. Micah, Layne, and the bunny all stared at each other.

Layne pointed at the bunny. "I know you want to ask me about Louis here, so go ahead."

"Louis?"

"Louis the rabbit."

Micah sipped his drink. "Okay, sure. Maybe I'm a little curious why you have a giant stuffed bunny named Louis."

"That's understandable. My daughter turns three next week, and today was the only chance I had to get her a present. The next few days are going to be jam-packed with work and other crap. So, here we are."

"Right," Micah said. "You have to get your bunnies while there's still time. I think that's an ancient Greek proverb."

Layne took a big slug of his coffee, glanced at Louis the rabbit, and chuckled. "Bunnies reaping what they sow. That's the way I heard it."

He laughed from his chest and his shoulders bounced

up and down as the laugh grew. Layne's hearty sniggering made Micah smile, but he didn't know why.

Micah's coffee date spilled big chunks of his life story, his divorce, all about his kid who he rarely saw, his two tours in Afghanistan, his contract work helping corporations hire security teams and install security networks. As Layne described how he helped companies by hacking into the security networks to test them, Micah couldn't help but think of what an asset Layne could be. He could easily break into Nathan's private hangar at the airport.

Micah could pick locks, but he knew nothing about security systems like that place had. But he remained wary. He had trouble sometimes gauging how much to trust people. Even though he'd tried twice with no luck and it seemed like bringing Layne along was a no-brainer, something still gave Micah pause. That fear of letting people see him vulnerable. See him in need.

As Layne talked, Micah mostly listened. He'd thought Layne was going to be the strong, silent type, but he actually had a lot to say. Maybe the caffeine in his system was the cause, but Layne didn't have any trouble keeping the conversation going.

"Is it weird," Layne said, "meeting some guy you don't know for coffee?"

"Seems a little like a date, right?"

"I hear you. Once you're my age, everybody's all settled in with their roots and their families. But I'm on the road so much, I don't get time to meet people, and I haven't had a workout partner for a while. I'll bet you can handle yourself in the ring a little better than you claim."

"It's been a while since I laced up those gloves."

Layne nodded thoughtfully. "Never too late to get it back, man. Tell me about you."

Micah talked about working for Frank, his job as a skip tracer, but he kept his mouth mostly shut about anything pre-Denver. As per usual, he kept his earlier details vague. He mentioned Oklahoma, but not specific cities, no school details. WitSec had provided a fake history that Micah had been required to memorize, but he felt reluctant to bring up the particulars if he could help it.

He hated lying about his past, but he had to remind himself that it wasn't as selfish as it seemed to do so. He had a brother and a sister and two parents to protect. No one should ever be able to connect the McBriars to him.

"What do you like to do for fun?" Layne said.

"I work a lot."

Layne sipped his coffee, waiting for more.

Micah decided to test him with a personal detail. "Also, I'm in recovery. I've been sober a year, so I spend a lot of my free time in places like church basements, talking to other drunks in meetings."

Layne seemed unfazed. "A year, huh? That's quite an accomplishment. I was a wild one in my youth, but joining the military was a big turning point for me. Straightened me right up."

Most people had some kind of reaction to learning that Micah was in AA. But Layne had not even batted an eye. Maybe he had family or friends in the program. Maybe he was even in recovery himself, but for whatever reason, wasn't sharing it.

Micah wanted to trust this guy. Wanted to mention the airplane hangar and ask Layne for help. But he couldn't make his lips form the words. The risk was too big. Plus, he had no idea if Layne would even be cool with something like that. It was technically illegal, after all.

Micah didn't yet know which way Layne's moral compass was going to point.

~

After coffee, Micah breezed home to prepare for a visit to a different coffee bar, but this time not to consume more go-juice.

At a quarter to eight, he entered the Bardo coffee shop on Speer. Daisy was kneeling on a raised wooden platform in one corner, fiddling with a guitar amp. Flicking switches and adjusting knobs. A Martin acoustic guitar rested on a stand next to her, shiny and new-looking.

Micah wouldn't have picked the sunburst finish, but it was a nice guitar, regardless. Probably purchased with Nathan's money.

There were about a dozen people in the shop, including the baristas behind the counter. That was fine with Micah because crowds weren't his thing. At least Daisy wasn't playing a show at a bar. And he guessed with her only a couple months clean and off drugs, she probably was grateful she wasn't playing a bar gig, too.

No sign of Nathan or his twin Alec among the small crowd. No European gangster, either, so that suggested they weren't tailing her. Micah scanned the crowd for anyone suspicious, but he only noticed the usual assortment of coffee shop people. Hipsters in skinny jeans and flannel, people hunched over laptops, clacking at the keys.

Micah hadn't expected Nathan to show up here, but he'd held on to the possibility. Daisy hadn't wanted a bodyguard, and also, she believed that Nathan was out of town. But Micah knew better than to blindly assume the boyfriend would stay away.

Micah cleared his throat and she looked up, with a broad smile on her face. She'd covered her black eye with makeup, and he could barely tell it had been there. She rushed across the room and threw her arms around him.

"You came," she said. "I can't believe you're here."

"I'm always up for some local music," he said, trying to play it off.

She beamed. "I'm so nervous. I forgot how nervous I get."

"You're going to be great."

She kissed him on the cheek, which made his eyebrows raise. Then, she gripped his hand for a second and pointed at an empty table. "I have to finish setting up."

"I'll let you get to it, then."

In another half hour, she was ready to play. When she began her first song, the crowd had swelled to fifteen people.

Her guitar skills could have used some work, but she could shuffle through the chords without looking at her fingers too much. Her singing voice, though, was stellar. She had a soulful, pained tone that rasped a little whenever she rose into the higher registers. At times as thin as a spider web, other times she growled with a surprising intensity.

Micah couldn't sing for shit, so his curiosity flipped to awe in the first few minutes.

After a couple of songs, he even forgot to keep checking the front door to make sure that Nathan or Alec or the European didn't make an appearance.

Daisy played a dozen tunes, maybe an hour total. Micah recognized a few of the songs, and the rest might have been originals, but he couldn't tell. When she was done, she rested the guitar on the stand and gave a simple, "thank you."

A small smattering of applause among the crowd, which had ballooned to twenty-five strong. Pretty good for a coffee shop.

After she'd finished, she came straight to Micah. Her chest heaving. "Thank you. Thank you so much for coming tonight. It means a lot to me."

"You okay?"

The smile on her lips threatened to take over her face. She touched his arm. "The energy. I forgot how much I love it."

"You were great, Daisy. Your singing voice is outstanding and if you were nervous up there, I couldn't tell. I'm seriously impressed."

She blushed, and Micah felt a pulse of heat to his cheeks, too. She turned her head away like a shy little girl. Micah felt that rush of discovery, something he hadn't experienced in what seemed like a long time.

"Got any more gigs lined up?"

She shrugged. "Not yet. This was just a test to see how I would feel."

"And how do you feel?"

"Amazing."

He smiled and felt the small talk was coming to a close. Sighing, he started to think of what to say so he could back out gracefully.

"Do you want to come over to my place?" she said. "My sponsor gave me a new box of Oolong tea I haven't had a chance to try yet."

Micah agreed and they met back at her apartment, but they never got around to making that tea.

# CHAPTER SEVENTEEN

ON FRANK'S THIRD day of his stay in Summit County, he finally laid eyes on Zaluski. Frank had been almost ready to pack it in and drive back to Denver. Cut his losses and help Micah out with his damsel in distress investigation.

He spotted the bail jumper in the lobby of the Baymont Inn as Frank was coming down for breakfast. When the elevator doors opened, he heard a distinctly-European voice coming from the lobby. Then, Frank leaned out the elevator and caught a blip of Zaluski's face before quickly darting back into the elevator.

The teenage girl who'd descended from the third floor with Frank raised an eyebrow, then she averted her eyes and strutted into the lobby.

Frank wrapped a hand around the elevator's edge to keep the door from closing. Leaned forward slowly, inching his head out until he could make sure Zaluski wasn't looking his way. In the pictures Frank had been given from Zaluski's bondsman, he'd had long, flowing hair down to his shoulders. Now the head was shaved to stubble. Also, the bail jumper's face was cut up and bruised, but there was no mistaking him.

So he *had* stayed in the hotel. Must have had multiple rooms to use as decoys.

He was arguing with the woman at the front desk. With his roller bag in one hand, he gesticulated in large, violent sweeps of his arm with the other. The front desk woman was nodding, clutching a sheet of paper to her chest, her brow wrinkled. Biting her lip.

Fighting over his bill, probably.

If Zaluski wasn't careful, he was going to get hotel security called on him, then the cops. Then they would find out who he was, slap him in handcuffs, and that spelled no bounty for Frank.

Fortunately for Frank, the situation didn't escalate. Zaluski gave up his battle and paid his bill with cash, then he stomped toward the front doors, dragging his roller bag behind him.

Frank sprung into action, keeping step with Zaluski, but maintaining a reasonable distance. Part of him wanted to snatch the jumper as soon as he got the chance, but part of him wanted to see where the guy was going. Zaluski had been holed up in this mountain town for days on end for a reason. And so far, Frank hadn't been able to figure out what that reason could possibly be.

Out of the building, Zaluski didn't head right toward the parking lot, he veered left, back toward I-70. Made sense, since Frank knew Zaluski's Lamborghini wasn't in the lot. The luxury car had been MIA ever since Zaluski had discovered the GPS tracker Frank had attached to it.

Zaluski hoofed it along Lusher Court, the short access road that joined with Summit Boulevard, which led into the main part of town.

Frank had to be careful on this access road since there weren't cars or nearby buildings or people to use as cover. He wrapped his scarf around his face and tried to look as if he were meandering. His current position put him far back from Zaluski, but the jumper might turn and find Frank suspicious. That would ruin everything.

Thirty seconds into following, Frank realized he didn't have his handcuffs or zip ties with him. They were back in the room. This morning, he'd been expecting to go downstairs and find nothing but hash browns and eggs in the hotel restaurant.

If he returned to the room, he would lose the guy. But, if Frank stayed on him, how was he going to apprehend his target? Frank had his gun in his armpit holster, but he couldn't pull it out anywhere near a crowd. Plus, Zaluski would probably have a gun of his own.

Some jumpers, all you have to do is flash your bounty hunter license, and they come willingly. Frank knew it wouldn't work with Zaluski. Frank would have to creep up behind him, clang the handcuff on one wrist, and then drag him to the ground to get him under control. The surprise was the best advantage he had.

Going face to face with this guy, Frank would lose all of his leverage.

But he didn't have a choice. He wasn't willing to lose

sight of Zaluski, so Frank kept on him, matching his steps and keeping a reasonable distance.

As expected, Zaluski headed toward Main Street. Frank paced with him for almost a mile, and even simply walking this much at altitude was exhausting him. Fortunately, Zaluski paused at a bus stop to smoke a cigarette, and Frank had a chance to recover. If he had to wrestle with Zaluski to apprehend him, he didn't know if he'd be able to muster the strength.

He resumed the chase after Zaluski snubbed out his cigarette. But instead of venturing all the way down to Main, Zaluski stopped a couple blocks short, just as Summit Boulevard crossed a river. The bail jumper turned off the sidewalk and climbed down a cascade of rocks next to the bridge, his roller bag bouncing around behind him.

Frank paused. He had to let Zaluski move a little ahead of him first. But he didn't walk west along the river away from Summit, he turned back east, headed under the bridge.

Frank hustled to the river, and he jogged down the slippery rocks as quickly as he could. Stopped before he reached within eyesight of the underpass, then he dropped to his knees. He crept forward until he could sneak a look underneath the bridge.

There was Zaluski, standing with another man. Didn't take any time at all for Frank to recognize the man as Everett Welker, the racist detective who'd been following Frank yesterday.

And even stranger was that Everett wasn't putting handcuffs on Zaluski, even though he was a wanted man.

No, Everett took the roller bag from Zaluski and shook his hand. In exchange, Everett gave Zaluski a fat envelope.

This explained some of why Zaluski had been hanging around town when he had every reason to leave. And it meant something bigger was going on. What that could be, Frank had no idea.

CHAPTER EIGHTEEN

D OWN THE STREET from Micah's apartment sat Denver's Union Station, a railway depot and shopping area. There were always inordinate amounts of people coming and going. Micah liked to sit out front on a bench and observe the crowd, the business people rushing to meetings, the school-skipping teenagers hanging out, the homeless people begging dollars. Gave Micah the sensation of being with people without having to actually talk to them.

He had a strange feeling in his gut today. Last night, he'd slept with Daisy, and the whole thing had felt like floating through a dream. As they kissed in her apartment, he kept thinking of the black eyes they both shared. Daisy from her boyfriend Nathan, and Micah from that unknown European gangster outside the hangar. As the clothes fell off in chunks while they made their way to her bedroom, he wondered if doing this was going to ruin everything with the case he was working. But then, she slipped her hand inside his boxer shorts, and all logic leaped out the window.

After the sex, there had been an abrupt conversation about how she liked to sleep alone in her bed, not to take it personally, this was just her little quirk. Micah gathered up his clothes and took the elevator back to his condo. Head swimming. The after-effects of lust, confusion about his feelings for the woman.

He'd sent her a text earlier this morning, to tell her he'd had a great time. She hadn't responded yet. He tried not to dwell on it, but doing so hadn't worked. Had he texted too soon? He was terrible with these things.

A white guy with biceps nearly bursting out of his shirt crossed Micah's path, and he thought of Layne. How he was Micah's best hope of getting inside that hangar to find out what the Auerbach brothers were doing in there. And also, that Micah still felt a niggling tingle of doubt that asking Layne for help might be a bad decision. Micah wasn't willing to cross that line yet.

He could usually stand about twenty minutes of people-watching at Union Station before growing bored and then he'd wander somewhere nearby to hunt for food. Illegal Pete's if he was feeling burrito-ish, or maybe Snooze Diner, if he wanted breakfast.

Thinking of his options, his stomach was beginning to grumble when a slick blue suit filled his vision.

Micah looked up to see Gavin Belmont, US Marshal. The same man who had been Micah's government contact for his first year in Denver. Micah's handler. The same man who had procured a new social security card and drivers license for Micah, then helped him get the job with Frank. The same man who'd watched him like a hawk until Micah dropped out of WitSec because of the pressure. Because of Gavin's constant micro-managing.

Or maybe that was only Micah's interpretation of the events at the time. He'd been drinking then, and his perceptions were admittedly distorted. He knew that fact now, but his instincts still told him Gavin was not on his side.

"Hi, Gavin."

"Hi, Micah. Haven't seen you in a while."

"I know. That's why I dropped out of the program, so you wouldn't have to see me anymore. So we wouldn't have to see each other and we could live the rest of our lives in separate peace."

Gavin frowned and adjusted his sunglasses. "I see you still have your razor-sharp wit, so that's good to know." He tilted his head back toward Union Station. "I have a booth reserved at the Cooper Lounge. Come on, I'll buy you a drink."

"It's 9:30 in the morning."

"That never stopped you before."

Micah flexed his jaw. "I don't drink anymore."

Gavin leaned forward and placed his palm against Micah's forehead. Micah recoiled from the touch.

"I don't feel a fever," Gavin said, grinning.

"I'm not interested."

Gavin removed his sunglasses and slipped them into his breast pocket. "I'm impressed. I didn't think you'd ever be able to give up the drinking. But now, I need to ask you some questions, and you're going to cooperate. If you don't want a drink, you can have ice water. Have you had breakfast yet?"

Micah considered his options as his stomach yawned. He didn't think he had any legal obligation to follow Gavin anywhere. Aside from twice trying to break into a private hangar near the airport, he hadn't done anything illegal lately to give Gavin cause to arrest him.

And if Gavin wanted to arrest him, he'd send cops. He wouldn't show up in person. This visit was for something else, so Micah didn't feel any immediate sense of danger.

Micah stood and waved an impatient hand toward Union Station. Gavin laughed and crooked a *follow me* finger while he walked away.

As Micah followed that blue suit into the building, he flashed on their last conversation. Micah had been drinking then, in and out of sobriety during his first year in Denver. He'd confronted Gavin and demanded he be released from WitSec. His handler, furious, warned him that leaving WitSec wasn't a license to go back to his old criminal ways. Threatening that if he put even one civilian life in danger, Gavin would personally break both of his legs.

So Micah wasn't too thrilled about whatever Gavin was going to say to him inside the Cooper Lounge. But he agreed because he wanted to get the unpleasantness over with.

Micah knew that he had changed a lot in the last year, but Gavin couldn't know that. He still didn't know the real Micah.

Inside the lounge, Gavin directed him to a secluded booth in the back. They sat. A little candle in a glass burned at the center of the table. There were two ice waters waiting for them, and Micah freed the plastic drinking straw from his glass and twirled it between his fingers.

"Okay, Gavin, let's hear it."

Gavin sipped his ice water. "I got pinged yesterday that you visited a police station up in Boulder. I spoke to a detective there who said you were belligerent. He said he was an inch away from restraining you and tossing you in a cell overnight to let you calm down."

"That's bullshit."

"Is it?"

Micah took a deep breath to steady his tone. "Those cops are dirty. Maybe a couple of them, maybe all of them, but something's not right with the police in this town."

"You people always claim police corruption," Gavin said, sighing. "It's like I can pull a string coming out of your ass and you play a recording from a microchip hidden inside your throat."

"You can believe whatever you want. I haven't broken any laws that you can prove, so you can't have me arrested. You told me to keep my nose clean, and I have. Everything else is academic."

Gavin raised his hands. "Old wounds, I get it. But can we take it down a notch? I know you always hated me, Micah, and I get why. But you should know that I tried to do my best for you. I was under a lot of pressure from the people in charge back then."

Maybe Gavin was right about that, but Micah couldn't help but lash out. "What do you want? I mean, really. Why are you here?"

"We want you to rejoin the program. Relocate. We've had a lot of management shuffling lately, and things are different. It's not like it used to be, all haphazard and complicated."

*Relocate.* Leave Frank, leave Denver, leave all the people he'd come to know in the AA meetings here. His adopted home. Abandon it all and start over again in some new city, with a new name on a new social security card.

"Why in the world would you want me back?"

Gavin sucked in a breath. "Your old employer, the Sinaloa, has had a resurgence lately. We think you can still be of some use in identifying them, and we need you not dead to make that happen."

"Not interested."

Gavin opened his mouth, then he caught himself. He removed a business card from his pocket and slid it across the table. "Will you think about it?"

"My life isn't perfect, but it's my life. I'm just now starting to get used to it. You want me to leave everything I've built and start over again? You've been you your whole life. You don't know what it's like to have to become someone else, permanently."

"Maybe so, but sooner or later, you're going to make a mistake. One of your old buddies from the cartel is going to see a picture of you on Facebook and show up here so he can cut you into tiny pieces. Your family, too."

Micah seethed. "Maybe if your people had given my

whole family protection from the start, I wouldn't have to be worried about them being hurt now."

Gavin sat back, reflecting. "It doesn't always work that way. And it's too late to bring them in now."

"So you're saying if I come back to WitSec, there's still no room for my parents? For my brother and sister."

Gavin shook his head.

"Then to hell with you."

Gavin stood and buttoned his suit. "Fine, Micah, if that's how you want it, but this offer won't be on the table for long. Go ahead and have breakfast on me. And keep your nose clean and your head down."

Gavin left, only his plain business card as a remnant of his presence. Micah picked it up. He held it near the candle's flame, not sure if he should burn it or stick it in his pocket.

# CHAPTER NINETEEN

NATHAN STOOD BESIDE his car at the rest stop in the little mountain village of George-town, a mid-way point between Denver and Frisco. Wasn't much of a town, really, more like a visitor center and gift shop supported by tourists getting gas on their way up to the real mountain destinations. A blip along the side of I-70.

Nathan blew into his hands to warm them as Alec's car pulled into the rest stop and parked a few spots down from his. A litter of small children all tumbled from the side of a minivan across the lot, and Alec eyed them from inside his car. Wouldn't get out.

Nathan gave a pointed sigh and implored his brother to leave his damn car. The minivan crew didn't even look in their direction.

Alec waited until all the kids and their parents had gone inside the visitor center, then joined Nathan. "You should be more careful."

"And you worry too much," Nathan said, slugging his brother in the shoulder. "It's just some church group or whatever in a minivan."

"It's so like you to be careless."

Nathan rolled his eyes. "Fine. You're right, Alec. You're always right. Now, what couldn't you tell me over the phone?"

"Were you busy?"

"Uh, yeah, obviously I'm busy. You should be, too. Z and that asshole detective from Denver are like two rabid dogs, and I'm doing everything I can to keep them from tearing each other's heads off. Managing people is not my strong suit."

"It will be over soon."

"I know, Alec. And I'm trying to get back to making that happen, so why did you get me out here?"

Alec sighed. "Daisy's upstairs neighbor, a guy named Micah Reed, went to the police yesterday."

"So?"

"He mentioned your name and said he wanted to report a crime. He didn't get into details, but it was enough to raise some eyebrows. It's contained in Boulder, but has obvious ripple implications."

Nathan braced his abs and dug his fingernails into his palms. "How does this guy know my name?"

"It's not hard to imagine how, living in the same damn building as her. She must have reached out to him."

"Okay, that's fine. She barely knows anything, and believe me, I put the fear of God into her before I left town. Tell me why we should care."

Alec opened his mouth to speak but paused when two of the children raced out of the visitor center, dancing and singing around the parking lot. Alec pointed at a spot in the ditch nearby, away from the minivan. Nathan waved his hands in surrender and let Alec lead him away. Although, it had to look more suspicious for two men to be conversing in a ditch next to the highway rather than in a parking lot. Cars rushing by, ankle-deep snow.

"You were saying?" Nathan said.

"Daisy may be clueless, but Reed is not. He works for a bounty hunter ex-cop. Maybe we could have played it off before, but our contact at Boulder Police accidentally mentioned her when he was asking Reed some questions."

Nathan tilted his head back and let a cone of steam out from his lips into the crisp air. "That fat idiot. I can't come back to Denver right now, so can you handle this?"

"Of course. Anything specific you want me to do?"

"Just keep an eye on him. If it looks like he knows anything or he's going to make trouble, then deal with it. We're so close to this being over. I'd rather not leave a mess behind in Denver if you can help it. But if this guy wants to insert himself, then that's on him. Be clean about it, and don't leave anything traceable behind."

"Understood," Alec said. "And Daisy? What do I do about her?"

Nathan paused. "I really don't want to kill Daisy unless we have to. Can you just… keep her busy? Find a way to distract her or something?"

Alec nodded. "I got it. I know exactly what to do about Daisy."

# CHAPTER TWENTY

I N THE EARLY afternoon, Micah decided he was going to find a way into Nathan's hangar, no matter what it took. As he sat in his car, parked at the gas station across the road, he was running out of options. He needed access to that building, pronto. Every day that slipped by was another chance the brawling European gangster might do something with DNA scraped from the cap Micah had dropped after fleeing their last fight.

So he needed access, but he had to get in stealthily. If that weren't a requirement, he'd drive his Honda right through the wall like an action hero. Then, he'd leap out of the open window of his car, bellowing a war cry and laying the insides to waste with automatic weapons fire.

Maybe not the last part.

He'd rather the Auerbach brothers not know anyone had been inside. And for that, he needed Layne, his new friend. As much as Micah dreaded putting himself in a position of asking for help, he didn't see how he had any other choice.

No one had been in or out of the building for as long as he'd been monitoring it from his car, across the street. He'd been here a full hour, so now was the perfect time.

Micah's hand shook as he sent Layne a text. His heart pulsed in his chest, higher and higher as he tapped out the words in his request. He felt embarrassed for being so awkward about all this.

In a few minutes, the phone buzzed.

"Hey, Layne."

"What's up, man?"

"I need to ask you a favor. Are you busy right now?"

"At the moment, no, not even a little. I've got a job up in Cheyenne in a couple days, so I'm killing time until then. Watching some stupid show on Netflix that I hate, but I can't seem to stop watching it. What's on your mind?"

"Something I'd rather discuss in person."

"Um," Layne said, "okay. We can do that. Meet me at the boxing gym in a half hour."

Micah hung up, and just like that, he'd committed to at least asking Layne if he would be up for this. A bead of sweat formed on Micah's temple. He was doing this. He was going to have to put himself out there and trust someone, for no good reason other than a hunch that this virtual stranger was okay.

Micah did things like this about as often as he slept with people he barely knew. He'd already done that particular rarity once this week, so maybe this was the week for

Micah to do all the un-Micah things in his imaginary task scheduler.

He drove to the gym and waited until Layne pulled up on his Harley. The hog was like a rocket blasting down the street. When he killed the engine, a strange silence arose in the absence of the cacophony.

"Do you ever wear sleeves?" Micah said, pointing at Layne's exposed arms. "It's forty degrees outside."

Layne looked down at his arms, covered with tattoos. "Of course I wear sleeves, but not unless it's cold." He lifted a hand out into the air. "This doesn't bother me. Plus, the ladies like to see the merchandise."

He flexed, and they both laughed. Micah couldn't help but feel drawn to Layne, but he wasn't sure why. If Micah could sketch a rough outline of his ideal friend, the guy wouldn't have looked at all like Layne Parrish.

Micah swallowed hard, and he imagined himself spitting out the words. Took him a few seconds to put it in motion. "I need your help."

"Hit me with it."

"I need to do something illegal, for a good reason. And I can't do it alone."

Just getting the words out, Micah felt a little lightheaded. He waited an endless two seconds as Layne's neutral expression held.

"I'm listening," Layne said.

Micah spilled it all. Daisy coming to him for help, her story about seeing Nathan counting piles of money, her abject fear of him, Micah getting into the fight with the guy at the hangar. The cop in Boulder threatening him outside the police station. Basically, everything that had happened to him and around him over the last four days, except sleeping with Daisy and the visit from the US Marshal Gavin.

No way would Micah spill to Layne details about who he'd been before moving to Denver. Some things, he needed to keep private, for more than a few reasons.

Through it all, Layne sat on his Harley, stone-faced. He nodded at the right moments, held eye contact with Micah. He didn't interject or ask any questions.

"Here's what I'm picturing," Micah said. "When we break into this private hangar, we're going to find some hard evidence of something. Drug trafficking, most likely. Maybe counterfeit bills, maybe even some crazy shit like pirated bootleg Blu-Ray discs. They're moving something through that hangar, so there has to be evidence."

Layne grinned. "Bull semen."

"Excuse me?"

"There's actually a big black market demand for stolen bull semen. Don't ask me how I know this, but yeah. Bull semen."

Micah raised an eyebrow. "Seriously?"

"Seriously."

"Well, I kinda doubt that it's bull semen. Whatever happens, we're going to keep at it until we find some proof, and then take it to someone who can do something about it."

Micah stopped speaking, waiting for a reply. Layne breathed, then sucked through his teeth as he stared up at the sky.

"The boyfriend, Nathan. He gave this woman Daisy a black eye?"

Micah nodded.

And then, after another endless pause, all Layne said was, "alright. I'm in."

## CHAPTER TWENTY-ONE

FOR STEALTH REASONS, Micah had asked Layne to leave his Harley back at the gym. The bike was like a chainsaw on wheels, so they opted for transportation that wouldn't herald their arrival like a thousand screaming demons. So now, they both sat in Micah's Honda near the gas station across from the hangar. It still appeared empty, as it had earlier today.

"There she is," Micah said. "Nobody's been in or out all day, as far as I can tell."

"You got a screwdriver?"

Micah popped the glove box and unearthed a skinny flathead, then held it out to Layne. Layne shoved it in his back pocket.

"Let's do this," Layne said.

"Wait a second. Shouldn't we talk about strategy?"

"Right. We're going to go up there and I'll break inside. If anyone attacks us, I'll shoot them." Layne pivoted in his seat and lifted up his shirt to show Micah a giant pistol sticking out of his waistband. Colt .45 Peacemaker.

"You walk around with that thing in your waistband?"

"You're goddamned right I do," Layne said, without a trace of irony. "I'm ready to go. Are you?"

Micah paused. "Why are you doing this with me?"

Layne sucked in a long, slow breath through flared nostrils. "I used to listen to my mother crying herself to sleep at night. I'm sure she thought I couldn't hear her, but the walls were so thin in that shitty apartment. My father…"

Layne trailed off, then thrust his chin to one side to pop his neck. "It doesn't matter. We focus on what's ahead of us."

Layne's confidence gave Micah a little boost. He'd been to this hangar twice already with no luck, so maybe Layne was the missing factor.

They strolled across the parking lot, keeping eyes on the building. No cars, no sound, no motion. Micah pointed to the back corner where he'd seen the door with the security panel.

Layne walked with his hands at his sides, not swinging his arms at all. Fists balled. Micah felt like a guitar string over-tuned to the snapping point, while Layne was a horse with blinders. Focused. Moving in a straight line.

When they stopped in front of the security panel, Layne rubbed a hand under his chin and nodded at the thing. "Okay, I know this brand. I think I can handle this."

He used the screwdriver to pop off the panel, and he tugged at a collection of wires coiled inside. He fingered through sets of red, blue, and green wires. Separated the blue ones, then yanked on them to move them away from the others.

"You know what to do with all that?" Micah said.

"Oh, for sure, no trouble, man. The only problem is, if they've done some kind of software modification, there's no way for me to know. According to the specs for this panel, I cut these blue wires, and we should open right up. But I can't promise they haven't reversed it."

Layne slipped the Colt from his waistband and held it out to Micah. "When I cut this, one of two things is going to happen. The door will unlock, or a screeching alarm is going to blast our eardrums. Either way, we might find people on the other side of this door. You know how to shoot that thing?"

Micah opened the cylinder and checked the bullets, even though he could tell by the weight that it was loaded. Heavy gun, at least thirty years old. But it wouldn't jam. It wouldn't accidentally fire because pulling these triggers required effort.

"I'm good," Micah said as he lifted the weapon at the door.

Layne held the point of the screwdriver against the wires and paused. "Try not to shoot me."

Layne severed the wires.

Nothing happened.

Then, a second later, the door clicked.

"Still might be a silent alarm," Layne said. "I wouldn't want to be here any longer than three minutes, tops."

"Then we should hurry," Micah said as he pulled back

the door, keeping the gun raised. Inside was a pristine white room, enormous and mostly empty. Shining painted concrete underfoot. No airplanes in the grand open space. A self-contained office room off to one side with stacks of something next to it. A few tool benches, but it seemed oddly barren for an airplane hangar.

They didn't flip on the lights, but enough sunlight filtered in through skylights from up above that Micah could see the whole room at once. Layne's footsteps echoed off in another direction, and Micah crept toward the office in the back.

"Shit," Layne said.

Micah spun to find Layne near one of the back walls, with one foot out in front, frozen in place.

Layne pointed down at the floor, and Micah squinted. Layne's foot was on a section of concrete that had sunken a half inch into the floor around it.

Micah dropped to his knees and crept next to it. "Pressure panel. What do you think happens if you lift your foot?"

Layne glanced all around him. "I don't see anything hanging above my head, and I don't think there's a hidden rifle attached to a string at the other end of this panel. I bet it's a failsafe."

If Layne lifted his foot, the alarm would trigger. Made sense. Micah considered some options, but nothing sounded good enough. He could try to put something heavy in its place, but he would have to maintain the same amount of pressure during the switchover.

"Whatever you're going to do, hurry up," Layne said. "I

can feel this thing jiggling under my foot. If I press too hard or too soft, I'm going to activate it."

An idea popped into Micah's head. "You still got that screwdriver?"

"Back pocket."

He reached around Layne's body and pulled the small flathead from his pocket. Micah dropped to the floor and examined the depression in the concrete. There was a tiny crack between the floor and the sunken panel.

"Here goes," Micah said, and he jammed the point of the screwdriver into the meager opening. He worked the handle back and forth to wedge the point into the crack, then when he let go, the screwdriver stuck straight up. The tension would keep the panel pressed down.

"We good?" Layne said.

"I think so, but there's no way to know without trying. Lift your foot off the thing and we'll see."

Layne took a breath and stepped off, and the sunken panel stayed in place.

"Nicely done, man," Layne said. "Sorry about that. Rookie mistake. You can see I'm out of practice."

"It's okay."

Layne pointed at the screwdriver. "You should probably wipe it for prints."

Micah nodded and wiped the cuff of his shirt on the handle of the screwdriver to clean it. He couldn't seem to avoid leaving his possessions in or near this hangar.

"Good idea. So much for leaving no trace, though."

"Too late to worry about that now. Let's get on with it."

They crossed the hangar toward the office, their footfalls reverberating and bouncing off the tall ceiling. As Micah neared the office, he could now tell what those stacks were. Coolers, the kind you pack with drinks and food.

"Got something there," Layne said, pointing at the stacks.

Micah gave the Peacemaker back to Layne and knelt in front of one of the coolers. Opened the one closest to him. Empty. Clean inside. He opened the second one and found it also empty. Then the next. Every single one he opened looked as if it had never been used before.

"Not what you were expecting?" Layne said.

"This doesn't make any sense."

"Maybe this hangar isn't the drop-off point. Maybe they fly out of here, down to Mexico or Columbia, or wherever."

"Maybe," Micah said as he returned the opened coolers back into stacks, as they were when he found them.

He hustled to the closed office room, which had a traditional lock. "I got this one."

Micah knelt, snatched his lock picking kit from his back pocket, and had the door open in ten seconds.

"Impressive," Layne said as Micah swung the door open. "You learn that in skip tracing school?"

"Something like that."

Micah didn't look up to see Layne's reaction. Layne didn't need to know where Micah had learned lock picking and other legally questionable skills. Didn't need to know anything about the Sinaloa cartel.

Inside the small room were two desks, each with their

own high-backed office chair. One for Nathan, one for Alec, no doubt. The walls were lined with framed maps, with a couple of file cabinets shoved into the corners.

Layne put his gun away and checked out the file cabinets. Micah dug into the desks, easily opening the locks on the drawers. He found mountains of paperwork, but nothing that told him, at a glance, what he was looking for. Purchase receipts for fuel and airplane parts. Flight logs. Cargo manifests full of lists of harmless items. None of it meant anything to Micah.

"Hey," Layne said. "Check this out."

Micah joined him by the file cabinet, where Layne was holding a stack of papers. "This address keeps popping up on a lot of these receipts. Seems our boys have been making deliveries here. You know this place?"

The address was in Broomfield, twenty minutes from Denver. Not too far from where Frank and Micah had apprehended a dangerous bail jumper about a year before.

"I know the area."

Layne opened his mouth to speak, but stopped short when his phone buzzed. He wrenched it free from his pocket. He stared at a message or email for a moment, then he sighed through clenched teeth. His eyes flicked to Micah and then back to the phone. "Shit. I have to go, man. I need you to take me back to my bike."

Micah shrugged and said that was fine, because, with the Broomfield address in hand, he knew what to do next. But something in Layne's evasive glances didn't sit right with him.

~

*INSIDE WITSEC BLOG*
*POST DATED 10.17*


*Mark Klosterman. Phil Criselli. Julianna Birosto. Michael McBriar. Tobin LaCosta. These are the names of some very bad people who were arrested and agreed to testify against their former employers in exchange for Witness Protection. Over the next several posts, I'm going to expose every one of them. Tell you their real names and where they live.*

*Julianna Birosto was known as the "ice queen" because she once killed a man by locking him inside a freezer. Didn't shoot him or strangle him or let him go out in any dignified way. She clubbed him over the head (from behind, even) and dragged his body into a cold storage freezer, then locked the door behind her. Cops found his body days later, in the fetal position, right behind the door.*

*Julianna was a trigger puller for an Irish mob out of Delaware (seriously. I had no idea there was mafia in Delaware until I read this article), and she got caught for the murder. Instead of doing life in prison, she agreed to five years in the penitentiary and then WitSec in exchange for testimony.*

*When she got out, she moved to Florida and lived under the name Shawna Hale. She didn't return to a life of crime or anything, but the thing is: Julianna didn't bring her family with her. She was on bad terms with them, so she left them behind.*

*And the Irish mobsters killed them all, in terrible, terrible ways. She had a little half-sister who was only sixteen years old. Her sister was torn to pieces by wild hogs, and her pieces were tossed from an overpass on I-95.*

*All because Julianna didn't like her family enough to save them.*

*Even though I've exposed her new name here, it won't matter. Julianna was killed in a car accident four years after moving to Florida (drunk driver. Karma is a bitch, right?) and it seems there was no foul play involved at all. Just one of those random things that happens in the universe.*

*Mark Klosterman was a low-level "enforcer" for the mafia in Chicago. He was an immigrant who became a citizen of the United States, took the oath like everyone else, and then crapped all over this country. In his police interviews, he claimed that he moved to the US from Germany specifically because of Al Capone. He wanted to be a big time gangster. Instead, what he ended up doing was breaking the thumbs of drug dealers who couldn't pay for the coke and heroin they'd been fronted. This big-timer eventually realized he was going nowhere, so he turned himself in to the cops and gave testimony in exchange for immunity.*

*So maybe you think, okay, so Klosterman's not so bad, right? After all, he gave himself up and did the right thing. Mark Klosterman (who is now living in Utah under the name Mark Jenner) murdered two people. A single mother and her child. Guess when that came out? After he'd been granted full immunity, of course.*

*Mark Jenner is walking around as a free man. If you live in Utah, maybe he shops at the same grocery store as you. Maybe he has been sitting next to you in a movie theater. Let that sink in for a moment. Then maybe you find out where he lives, and if you live in that same neighborhood, you consider moving.*

*Coming up next post: more real names of horrendous people who got an undeserved second chance.*

# CHAPTER TWENTY-TWO

~

MICAH SPENT SOME of the afternoon in his condo, thinking about Layne's strange expression when he'd received that text message and then said he needed to go. Micah was so used to being suspicious and wary of people, he assumed there was something Layne wasn't telling him.

Eventually, he decided that there very well might be something Layne wasn't telling him. And that didn't necessarily make Layne's secret nefarious, only something that was none of Micah's business.

Making friends with regular people was a weird proposition. Back when he was drinking, he usually maintained friendships only with those could keep up with him. Anyone who didn't party as hard as Micah would be deemed a *lightweight* and would be cut from the social circle. Or, they could stay if they had good drug connections. Micah had been a drinker, but he liked to dabble in the other stuff from time to time.

Then, in the Sinaloa cartel, he'd been paired with his only true, longtime friend Phillip Gillespie, who Micah had always called Pug. Pug had long since earned Micah's trust to become the kind of person who always watched his back.

The kind who had died because of Micah.

As Micah became increasingly comfortable in sobriety, Pug entered his thoughts less frequently. But like athlete's foot, the pain and guilt seemed to creep up again and again.

A notification on his phone informed him of the newest blog post on the *Inside WitSec* blog. Standing in his kitchen with a bag of potato chips in one hand, Micah read, and panic gripped him. Seeing the name he'd been born with displayed online troubled him in more ways than one.

*Michael McBriar. Born in Oklahoma, dropout of Oklahoma State University, died in a car crash. Except not really.*

Sure, a few people knew his secret. And probably many more didn't believe the rumors that had been spread that he'd actually died in that car crash after the trial. But he didn't want his parents to see this blog post. Didn't want to give them the hope that Micah might still be alive, since he couldn't ever contact them again.

But he had no control over whether or not they would see it.

The pressure gave him the tiny fire of a yearning for a drink. Not a craving or a compulsion, only that irksome pest of an idea that it would make things better.

"Doesn't make anything better," he said as he slipped his phone into his pocket.

Reading this blog wasn't going to help, either.

Micah tried not to think about it as he waited for dark so he could drive to Broomfield and investigate the address he'd found at the hangar. After the sun had sunk behind the mountains to the west in a flaming burn of pink to purple, he drove his old Honda Accord up Highway 36 and exited in Broomfield, the same exit he'd take to reach A1 Lawnmower Repair. A1 was owned by the same man who owned the Pink Door strip club downtown. Burly Tyson Darby with the banana-shaped scar under his eye. Micah wondered if the proximity could be a coincidence. Possibly, but he wouldn't be shocked if that crooked club owner was involved in all this somehow.

The strip club was down the street from Glazer's gym, where he'd met Layne, who had helped Micah get access to this address in Broomfield. Funny how things sometimes circled back.

Micah parked a block away from a warehouse that matched the address discovered at the hangar. One of the companies Nathan consulted for owned this building. No big surprise there.

He felt his first whiff of hope since nothing had led him anywhere close to Nathan Auerbach so far. Dead ends and obstructions. If this warehouse had some connection to however Nathan was making his money, Micah would hunt until he found it.

Tonight. No more messing around.

The warehouse lived among a set of office buildings,

like a complex. It ran for almost half a block, with a big glass building out front that connected to a large concrete structure with several loading bays for trucks.

Somehow, Nathan was moving his drugs through here, which was linked to the private hangar by the airport. Inserting them into harmless-looking boxes of air fresheners, then a few would fall off the truck and find their way into that hangar?

That was a reasonable explanation.

In the small parking lot out front, Micah counted three cars. A warehouse like this might have day and evening shifts, so he needed to avoid venturing into any main area. The tinted glass of the building out front shielded the insides, so Micah didn't dare start there. No, he was looking for something through one of the loading bays, maybe an unused bay around the back, maybe something in a hidden location not easily accessible.

Micah left the car, armed with a set of lock picks and the new hunting knife he'd bought online. He slid the knife into its sheath and slipped that inside his socks. Tested walking around the car to ensure it wouldn't fall out. He switched his phone to silent and then headed around the complex to find a way to access the loading bays.

There were no locked gates since trucks would need to come and go freely. With the massive concrete building on his left and a neighborhood street on his right, he casually walked down an open alley with an attached sidewalk. Wasn't exactly public property, but he could get away with wandering here if someone came by to question him. *Oh, hello, security guard. Just looking for my dog that ran away. Yes, I live in that neighborhood over there.*

Micah counted six loading bays down this never-ending alley until he finally found one that was smaller, part of a separate structure next to the main warehouse building. And this loading bay was boarded up.

"And we have a winner," he said as he touched the nub of Boba Fett's head in his pocket. Micah approached, cautiously listening for sounds emanating from inside the building. Seemed all quiet. On the sidewalk, he could feign innocence, but if he were lurking near or in the building, no excuses would get him out of a trespassing charge.

There was a small door next to the loading bay, also boarded up. Sign taped to the piece of particle board over the door: *Warehouse E Not In Use.*

Micah examined the particle board. Where it had been attached to the wooden door frame, the holes around the nails were scuffed and larger than necessary. Someone had repeatedly been removing this barrier over the door. So, they weren't transporting cargo out through the loading bay, they were doing it through this smaller door.

Micah slipped out his hunting knife to pry the nails from the particle board, then he removed it and picked the lock. He tested opening the door a couple inches to see if it would creak, but it moved silently.

He remembered the pressure plate booby trap back at the hangar. Had to be ready for anything.

Micah pushed the door open to a room the size of a large garage, but it was too dark to see anything. He paused, listened. Nothing came back. He shined his phone's flashlight around to see dusty concrete floors, metal shelving in rows, boxes on those shelves. The density of the shelves left little room to maneuver around them. Just some small pathways snaking from one side of the room to the other.

Not much else was here, aside from a couple of tables with shrink wrap rolls and cutting devices. Pallet wrapping material.

He checked a box on one of the shelves, but it contained only styrofoam peanuts. Same with the next box. And the next. Every box he checked contained the same pedestrian, non-drug trafficking non-surprises.

Micah gritted his teeth. What was he supposed to do? This had to be the place.

He shined the flashlight around the floor, checking the dust. Squinting, he looked back at his path around the room and noticed a set of footprints that didn't look like his. They were so faint he could barely make them out. He followed the hint of footprints to the far side of the room, terminating at the wall. Dead end.

Except, when he shined his flashlight, he could make out dark lines slicing up through the drywall, and at about halfway up, some indentations on either side of the crack. Like little half-domes pressed into the plaster.

Finger holds.

He held the flashlight low and pressed into those indentations to find a grip, and he pulled back the plaster. It creaked and a mist of drywall dust burst into the air as Micah wrenched open the improvised door cut into the back wall.

There was another room through this passageway.

Micah killed the flashlight and opened the drywall door enough to step through. This room was cooler, and too dark to see anything clearly. He noticed a distinct scent right away. Something antiseptic, mixed with a rusty and metallic smell.

He stilled his breathing and listened until he was certain no one was in this room with him. Then he turned on his flashlight and gasped when his eyes adjusted to the light.

He was standing on a tile floor, and he could see a line of blood streaked across the tile. Some of it was fresh, running along a path toward a drain a few feet from Micah. The walls were white, barren. But he couldn't see the whole of the room because there were dividers set up. Large, wire-framed dividers with wheels, and fabric hanging from the tops of the frames. Kind of like the cloth dividers in rooms at hospitals, except mobile due to the wheels. There were two dividers in front of Micah running from each wall, with a small path in the middle.

Beyond that path was darkness.

Micah walked toward the break in those two dividers, his phone in one hand and the knife in another. He took extra care to avoid stepping in any of the blood on the floor. No footprints.

He reached the divider and leaned forward, looked left first. There, he saw a mattress on a metal frame, also with wheels at the base. Like a cot, almost. He glanced right and saw another one like it. The sourness of the smell became more distinct back here. Blood, and lots of it.

He inched toward the cot, positioned next to a cloth-covered table. On the table sat a pristine stainless steel tray and a bucket on top of that tray. Micah peered into the bucket and found a bloody bandage.

He gagged as he realized what he was looking at, and then had to turn his head for a moment to catch a breath. Blood spatters colored the sheets on the cot. He checked the other bed. A tray on a stand next to it housed scalpels, saws, other stainless steel implements. One saw was like a semi-circle with handles at each end, and a serrated edge. Crusted, black blood lined the edge of the blade.

A bone saw. This saw had been used to cut someone's limbs off.

He was starting to get the idea that Nathan and Alec Auerbach weren't into the drug trade. This was something else entirely, but Micah's brain couldn't fully process all of this information.

What the hell was this place?

Heart pounding, stomach gurgling, Micah left the bed and proceeded to the second row of dividers. He gulped huge breaths as he crossed, and turned right first this time.

On this bed was a body, mostly covered with a sheet. He jumped and raised the knife. Let out a startled yelp. But the person on the bed didn't move. The chest did not rise and fall, the eyes did not flicker as Micah flashed his light over the face.

Micah focused the light on the body. A woman, maybe forties, but hard to tell. Definitely dead. Her skin was milky white, blue veins under the surface. Micah stepped closer, and he could feel blood underneath his shoes.

Heard the slick sound his feet made as they moved through it.

This woman had a hole in her side. A large, gaping, bloody hole.

Someone had removed something from her body. Kidneys, Micah guessed. Nathan wasn't into drugs at all, just as Daisy had argued. He was running some kind of probably-involuntary organ donor operation, right out of this makeshift surgery room.

Micah backed out of the pooling blood and grabbed a towel sitting on the table. He wiped off the bottom of his shoes and smeared his footprints next to the bed.

He raised his phone and snapped pictures of the tile, the surgical instruments, the bloody rags collected on the floor.

Near the back of the room sat a large freezer. Micah shined his light on it. Larger than a typical garage freezer, this thing was the size of a small car. And it had a keypad on the front of it.

Micah's head spun. But he didn't have much time to think about it, because as he finished taking pictures of the area, footsteps tapped behind him.

# CHAPTER TWENTY-THREE

**D**AISY LEFT WORK at five, which was as much of the coffee shop as she could stand that day. If she'd had to work a double or a split, she might have screamed at someone. One of those days where she'd promise herself that if things got bad enough, she'd quit. She probably wouldn't, but thinking like that helped her endure to the end of her shift.

She'd messed up a customer's latte that morning, had added a shot of vanilla instead of caramel. Simple mistake. But the guy yelled at her as if she'd done it on purpose. He'd berated her, made her feel stupid and weak and inadequate. Eventually, her manager came over and smoothed over the whole situation. He pacified the customer with a free drink coupon and hadn't given Daisy any punishment.

Even though her boss had been kind to her, that customer's harshness weighed on her for the rest of the day. How could people be so cruel?

As she rode the elevator to her condo, she realized none of that mattered. Tomorrow, she was going to spend time with her son. To finally see Caden after he'd been with his dad for six straight weeks. And that was worth more than all the latte-swilling assholes in the world. So the rest of the day would be spent cleaning, re-inserting all the little plastic plugs into the electrical outlets. Converting her two-bedroom apartment into a home, if only temporarily.

She opened the front door of her condo with a smile on her face until she looked down when her foot touched the corner of an envelope. Someone had shoved it under her front door. She bent and picked it up, trying to keep her hands from shaking. Didn't work.

No text at all on the front. But she had a feeling who'd left it here. She opened the unsealed envelope and withdrew a single sheet of paper.

> *D-*
> *You need to relax. Have some fun.*
> *-A*

No mystery here. The *A* was for *Alec*, Nathan's brother. Even before Daisy had become terrified of Nathan, she'd never felt comfortable around his twin. They were alike in many ways, but Alec never smiled. Never cracked a joke or found other people's jokes funny. Nathan's sense of humor had won over Daisy from their first date. Alec was like a dog always on the verge of growling.

But the problem with him was much more basic than that. His name. Alec.

It was too close to Alex, which was Daisy's brother's name. The name was too much of a reminder of the sibling she'd lost for no reason at all. Alex Cortez, former straight-A student and standout third baseman for his little league team.

Alec looked nothing like Alex. One was tall with black hair, brown eyes, and pale white skin. The other was short and skinny with brown skin. But she never wanted to be made to think of that name against her will. Didn't want to dredge up those feelings which were like kicks to the gut, every time it happened. Every time someone said "Alec," the word blindsided her.

Too painful. She missed her brother too much.

At least, when she was on drugs, she didn't have to think about it. Now, clean and sober for over two months, she didn't have any medication to kill the mourning inside her. Facing the world straight every single day was a daunting task.

Daisy read the note a couple times, unsure what it was supposed to mean. Since it had come from Alec, Nathan was probably still out of town, but no mention of where. No texts or calls from either of them.

She considered texting Micah, to let him know Nathan was still gone but that Alec had made contact. But, she couldn't bring herself to tap Micah's contact info on her phone. She hadn't talked to him since they'd slept together, and she didn't know how to begin to communicate. Last night had been a mistake.

She kept doing this to herself. Making bad decisions, seeking dangerous activities she knew she'd regret later. Why couldn't she resist these stupid urges that drove her to act like such a heel? Even two months sober, she was still doing it.

She opened her laptop to waste some time, but her favorite horoscope website wouldn't load. Her fingers drummed on the keys, growing impatient. With a sigh, she opened the Mac terminal and ran a traceroute to find out why it was running so slow, but she didn't have the patience to wait for that, either. She tossed the laptop on the couch next to her.

Her eyes fell back to the envelope.

*Have some fun.*

Daisy carried the note and the envelope to her couch, and she tossed them both onto the coffee table. As she did, a tiny Ziploc baggie flew out of the envelope and landed on the carpet. The thing was no bigger than her thumb.

She bent and scooped it up from the floor.

Cocaine. She flicked a finger at the baggie and it danced, pinched between her fingers. About a gram inside, enough to keep her going for the rest of the day. Enough to give her a few of hours of thinking that everything was right with the world and she had no problems worth caring about.

Until, of course, she would come down and realize that she'd tossed sixty-six days of sobriety into the garbage bin. Then she'd have to get clean all over again, if that were even possible. Her last bender was supposed to be a weekend of fun, but it had turned into a month of drug-fueled bad decisions and chaos. Lucky that she'd kept her job through the whole debacle.

*You need to relax. Have some fun.*

Daisy held the bag in her hand, used her fingers to scoot it around in her palm. How did this powder have such a hold on her? How could the desire for it make the backs of her knees sweat, her head swim, her stomach do somersaults on a trampoline?

It was poison, and she believed that truth wholeheartedly. She knew it could lead to death and yet she still wanted it. Even more, her body claimed she needed it. That she wouldn't be right without it. How was that possible?

Caden would be here tomorrow. This powder could ruin her last chance to see her son on a regular basis. She would become birthday cards and emails and never spend another night under the same roof as her own child.

She stood, gripping the baggie in her hands. She dropped the baggie on the coffee table, then picked it up again. Held it to the light, watching the tiny white grains shift inside their plastic prison. She bounced it in her palm a couple times, feeling the weight settle. It was only about as heavy as a nickel, but holding it made her wrist ache.

"Enough, Cortez," she said, and her voice sounded weak. She hated that.

Daisy walked into the bathroom, flushed the cocaine down the toilet, and the baggie with it. She placed a hand on the cool porcelain of the sink counter until her lightheadedness passed. Her fingers caressed the crucifix hanging from the chain around her neck.

Then, she proceeded to clean her apartment in anticipation of Caden's arrival.

# CHAPTER TWENTY-FOUR

MICAH WAS STANDING in the middle of this makeshift surgery room in the back of the warehouse when the lights blinked on around him.

Panic seized his thoughts. The bright overhead lights momentarily blinded him, and he couldn't think. This room had exactly one way out.

Then, his eyes adjusted, and he darted around, looking for a place to hide. With only a knife to defend himself, he didn't feel confident taking on someone who might have a gun. Whoever had come in would obviously kill to protect this place.

Micah's eyes landed on a metal cabinet sitting a foot away from the wall. Maybe three feet wide, but big enough to hide behind. He slinked toward it, wedging himself between the back of it and the wall. Kept his arms at his sides as he pulled his body out of view. If he bumped the cabinet and it budged, the thing might make noise. He had no idea what was inside the cabinet.

He tried to stay still and quiet because he barely fit behind the thing. If someone caught a good angle, they'd see him immediately. He tried to still his breathing. His exhalations spread out over the back of the metal cabinet, fogging it.

The footsteps neared, stopped, came closer. Micah tried to spy out of the side of the cabinet edge, and he could make out the outline of a shape through a fabric divider. The shadow of a large man, with an extended arm and a gun, clutched in that hand.

Micah passed the knife from his right hand to his left for a second so he could wipe his hand on his pants. Hiding behind the cabinet had made him vulnerable. If this guy spotted Micah from a distance, he'd have nowhere to run.

He considered bolting from his spot and crashing through the divider to topple the guy. But Micah had no means to know which way the guy was looking; he might be spotted before even reaching the divider.

Something chirped, like the squawk of a radio. A voice spoke, garbled and full of distortion. In a moment, the shape through the curtain tilted its head and mumbled something. He was talking into a walkie-talkie clipped to his shoulder.

This guy was a cop. But if he were here investigating the surgery, he wouldn't have come alone. This was not the good kind of cop. This guy already knew about this place, and he was making sure the room was unmolested.

The footsteps resumed, and the man passed the divider. Micah's jaw clenched. The chubby cop from Boulder County, the man with the mustache slug on his upper lip. The one who had talked about what a great *see-fop* donor Nathan Auerbach was.

Micah's anger swirled. He'd been right, and also not surprised in the slightest. Corrupt cops in the illegal organ trafficking trade? He wanted to knock over the cabinet and scream at the guy. But that was a quick way to eat a bullet, no doubt about that.

Micah thought of Layne, who never went anywhere without that oversized Colt Peacemaker in the back of his waistband. Micah used to carry a gun every day, but he didn't like to do that anymore. Yes, he'd pulled a trigger more than once since moving to Denver and becoming someone else, but he still didn't like it.

But this was one of those times he sure could have used a gun. Wished he had a little more of that old person still inside him.

Instead of revealing himself, he fished his phone from his pocket and snapped a quick picture while the cop's head was turned. Micah thought he'd caught enough of his face to identify him, but Micah didn't take the chance of checking now.

The guy began to pivot in his direction, and Micah pulled back behind the cabinet.

The cop had to be poking around because Micah had removed the particle board from the outside door. The cop would have suspected a break in. Possibly, he might be thinking neighborhood kids had messed with the particle board, but that cop intuition would tell him to check out the inside.

Micah hadn't stepped in the bloody trail at the front of the room. He hadn't left anything out in the open. The room should appear untouched.

The footsteps shuffled for a few seconds, and Micah didn't dare look out from his hiding spot. The sounds stopped, and the room grew quiet. His heart thumped in his chest.

Micah kept a close grip on the knife, ready to slash at anything that entered his view. He opened his mouth wide to force his breaths in and out at an even pace.

But the cop didn't come any closer.

In another minute, the footsteps resumed, growing lighter. Micah waited until the count of sixty, then he slipped out from behind the cabinet. He kept low, padding across the tile until he reached the exit to the main room of this side warehouse.

He stepped into the warehouse, and it was empty. The cop was gone.

Now alone, Micah checked his phone and scrolled through the pictures. The trail of blood showed up perfectly in the pictures, but the cop's face was turned. Couldn't make out any of his features.

Damn it. Wasn't good enough.

# CHAPTER TWENTY-FIVE

SINCE SPYING ON the meeting yesterday between racist detective Everett and bail jumper Zaluski, Frank wasn't sure which one of them to follow. If he'd had Micah here with him, they could split up and handle both at once. But the kid was back in Denver, handling that probably-no-big-deal thing for the pretty Latino girl with the bad boyfriend. Nathan What's-his-face. The guy counting the money, supposedly with cops.

Not that cops couldn't be corrupted. Everett Welker was evidence of that. For some reason, the detective hadn't arrested Zaluski when he'd had the chance under that bridge yesterday. The only reasonable conclusion was that the two of them were into something together.

A part of Frank wanted to call Micah and ask for his help, but maybe the kid needed to stick with his own thing in Denver. Maybe it would be good for him to take on this challenge and see it all the way through to the end.

Frank couldn't run the bond agency forever, and he needed to start thinking about what would happen when he retired. And Micah might not even be interested in running the business. He was only a year sober; he probably hadn't figured out what he wanted to do with his life yet. Sobriety has funny ways of making your priorities shift unexpectedly.

Frank shaved in the bathroom of his room at the Baymont. He was tired of forking over money for this place, but it would all be worth it if he could bring Zaluski back. Would be considered an on-the-job expense. Of course, if he didn't catch Zaluski, he would be out the money. Mueller Bail Enforcement couldn't handle too many losses this year, unless he wanted Micah to inherit nothing but a stinking pile of debt.

Had to get Zaluski. It was the only thing that mattered.

Frank supposed he could have nabbed the European yesterday, but he hadn't. The temptation of discovering him in league with a corrupt cop-especially one as offensive and slimy as Everett—was too much to pass up. Frank wasn't sure if that possibility was going to equal the potential of letting him slip away, though.

But Frank had learned where Zaluski was staying now, after having checked out of the Baymont. The Super 8 in Dillon, a couple miles back east along the interstate. So Frank was up at the crack of dawn, hoping to slink into that Super 8 before Zaluski was awake, and hoping to catch him doing something that could also bring down Everett. Break two boards with one punch.

Frank drove along the Dillon Dam Road instead of I-

70 so he could follow the lake the whole way. This late in October, there were no boats on the water, but it still hadn't frozen over yet. Just an endless expanse of silky blue with jagged, snow-capped peaks all around. Who wouldn't love these mountains?

A lot nicer than where Frank had grown up. He reminded himself of that fact whenever he slipped into self-pity mode.

He parked in front of the Super 8 and laid eyes on the gray Mercedes Zaluski had adopted since ditching his Lamborghini. The Mercedes was parked next to a flashy Aston Martin. Some kind of overpriced car collection going on here in the parking lot of the Super 8. These two cars stuck out like a church lady in a whorehouse.

Frank cautiously approached the motel and peeked in the lobby before entering. Didn't want to stumble on racist asshole detective Everett, since he would spot Frank in an instant. Through the glass doors, he could see the check-in area to the right, with a bank of desktop computers beside it. Straight ahead was a set of stairs, and to the left, a small breakfast nook area. TV on the wall, counters with cereal and bread, small collection of tables. A half-dozen people were in the breakfast nook area, pouring cereal and toasting bagels.

Zaluski was one of them.

Frank almost didn't recognize Zaluski at first, because he was wearing a blue baseball cap. The bail jumper was sitting at a circular table, stabbing a waffle with a knife and fork. No Everett in the vicinity.

Frank entered the building, careful to keep his head

down. Zaluski was sitting at a right angle, but he might spot Frank out of his peripheral. Frank had no reason to think the European had spotted him at any point in the last four days, despite the GPS tracker incident two days ago. Zaluski might have assumed any number of people would be out to get him and had planted it.

Still there was no use being careless, so Frank stayed out of sight. Taking little peeks when he could, he got a better look at the cap. A faded Denver Nuggets cap. Micah had one exactly like it.

Frank then noticed someone else familiar, sitting at the table across from Zaluski. Dark hair, blue eyes, tall and handsome white guy. In a second, Frank put it together. This was Nathan, the bad boyfriend, or his twin brother. He remembered the neighbor Daisy showing him and Micah a picture of them when she'd first come into the office. She'd said one of them had blue eyes, the other brown.

This one had the blue eyes. Nathan Auerbach.

So, Zaluski knew Nathan. Frank couldn't muster the energy to be surprised. Nathan was in some high-dollar illegal enterprise, and Zaluski was a known drug smuggler who was sticking around Colorado, despite being a wanted man. Made total sense that these two might have business together.

Frank wandered near the breakfast nook, pretending to look at a rack of pamphlets, with his back to his two targets. Rafting excursions. Mine tours. Guided snowmobile outings. He picked up one about a steam train ride in nearby Georgetown, flipped through it, bobbing his head.

But his ears were tuned toward Nathan and Zaluski, chatting while they were eating.

When Frank focused, he could pick out some of the words. Unfortunately, they weren't speaking English. He sneaked a pen from the inside of his coat pocket and scribbled on the pamphlet anything he could make out. Since he had no idea how to spell whatever the hell they were saying, he made his best guess.

The occasional English word popped into the dialogue, and Frank recorded those in a separate column. He didn't know how to make sense of any of this gibberish.

After about five minutes of scrambling to record as much as he could, Frank wandered away as Nathan and Zaluski got up from their seats. They dropped their plates in a bin next to the cereal station and strutted past the front desk, toward a back door.

Frank looked at all these meaningless words scribbled on the glossy pamphlet. How the hell was he going to figure this out?

# CHAPTER TWENTY-SIX

ICAH RECLINED ON his couch, scrolling through the photos on his phone. The warehouse pics were all sharp and clear. But, the picture he'd snapped the other day at the hangar of Nathan, Alec, and the European had been taken too far away to be useful.

The idea to get a cat suddenly popped into his head, for some strange reason. A dog wouldn't work; Micah often had to bolt at the drop of a hat to leave town. But all a cat needed was food and water and occasional attention. But then, he thought of vacuuming up all that fur and the stench of a litter box.

He removed Boba Fett's head from his pocket and set it on the coffee table. "You're all I need, Boba."

Boba Fett said nothing.

"Right," Micah said. "Back to work."

He had evidence that this cop—who was most likely in league with Nathan and Alec—was involved in the illegal organ donor trade. But what to do with this evidence? He didn't feel safe going to any cops. It wasn't possible that every cop in the metro Denver area was crooked, but Daisy had described seeing several of them with Nathan the night she'd witnessed him counting the money.

There had to be a way to use this evidence. Had to be a way to bring in someone from the outside who had the authority to expose all of the players in this organization.

As he was thinking about it, his phone vibrated. Call from Frank.

"Hey, boss."

"Hi, kid. I need your help."

"Of course. What can I do for you?"

Frank paused a second. "You okay? How are things going with your pretty neighbor investigation?"

"A lot of ups and downs. I was sure he was into the drug trade, but it's not that at all. Organ trafficking."

"Organs? Like hearts and livers and all that?"

"I'm fairly certain that's what's happening. I've found some evidence, but I'm not sure if it's enough to implicate Daisy's boyfriend Nathan yet."

"Speaking of the damn devil. Well, you're not going to believe this, kid. I've been up here in Frisco all week, tracking my mark Zaluski, when your guy Nathan Auerbach happened to show up to have breakfast with my bail jumper."

Micah didn't even pause at the mention of Nathan's name because he was too busy repeating the name Zaluski in his mind. Realization smacked him in the face. The European he'd scuffled with at the hangar. He'd chopped all his hair off, that's why Micah hadn't been able to place him that day. Frank had shown him pictures of a long-haired Zaluski when he took on this bounty job from another bondsman.

"That actually makes a lot of sense," Micah said. "I ran into Zaluski down here, four or five days ago. At a private hangar near the airport. We got into it."

"Well, that explains why his face is all cut up. I didn't spot him until yesterday morning, so he could have been in Denver before that. Speaking of him, when you two tussled, he didn't happen to steal your Nuggets cap, did he?"

Micah felt a smile creep over his face. A wave of relief. "Actually, he did. I accidentally left it behind when I was running away from him."

Good to know Micah didn't have to worry about that cap sitting in a crime lab somewhere, being tested for DNA. One less thing to obsess about.

Then he realized what Frank had said before. "Wait. Nathan is up in Summit County?"

"Yep. I was in the same room with him."

Daisy had said Nathan was going out of town, so Summit County must have been the destination. But why? Nathan, Alec, Zaluski, the corrupt mustachioed cop from Boulder. Were they all partners in the organ trade business?

"All these people are connected," Micah said.

"Looks that way."

"So what's going on, Frank? What do you need my help with?"

"I overheard the two of them talking, but it was in some foreign language. I wrote down a few of the words, but they were talking so fast, I mostly only got the things they'd said three or four times. I thought you told me one time you could translate stuff on the internet. Is that right?"

"Sure, I can give it a go." Micah opened his laptop and browsed to an online translation website.

Frank spelled out the words phonetically, and Micah wrote them down in a text file, just as Frank had described them.

*Senna*
*Zah-beach*
*Nair-kuh*
*You-trough notes*
*Spote-kahn-yuh*

Micah went to work, trying various combinations of how he thought the words would be spelled, based on Frank's descriptions. He started with *Senna*. Quickly found a Polish word (which made sense, given the name *Zaluski*) *cena*, which translated into English as "price."

The other words were *zabić*, *jutro noc*, *nerka*, and *spotkanie*.

"Okay, Frank, I think I got it. *Cena* is 'price,' *zabić* is 'kill,' *jutro noc* is 'tomorrow night,' *nerka* is 'kidney,' and *spotkanie* is 'meeting'. Does this mean anything to you?"

Frank sighed. "Maybe. A little bit of their conversation was in English, so I got some of that. They were discussing types of cheeses for almost a full minute. But, there was another word they were saying, I couldn't tell if it was English or not. But I think they were saying *Vail*. I'm pretty sure of it now."

A meeting in Vail. *Spotkanie jutro noc.* Meeting tomorrow, in Vail.

"There's going to be a gathering in Vail tomorrow night," Micah said. "Some kind of organ trafficking sale or a meeting."

"That explains a lot of this crap I've been seeing that doesn't make any sense." Frank breathed on the other end of the line for a few seconds. "I'll be damned. Seeing as how our investigations have crossed paths, think you can find your way up to Vail? Let's work this together."

"Of course, Frank. I have some things I need to take care of first, but I can be there tomorrow."

"No problem. We have time."

"I'll call you when I'm on my way."

Micah ended the call and stared at his phone as it darkened and then auto-locked. This cleared up some things, but not everything. He still had to solve the problem of the surgery farm at the warehouse in Broomfield.

And if all these assholes were either in Vail or on their way, now was the perfect time to deal with it.

# CHAPTER TWENTY-SEVEN

MICAH STOOD OUTSIDE Daisy's door, his hand in the air, ready to knock. But he couldn't make his arm finish the motion. They hadn't spoken since they'd slept together. A sticky, passionate coupling that had ended with Daisy saying she wanted to sleep alone in her own bed. Micah not knowing what to say as he gathered his clothes and left her bedroom.

But now, he was here on official business, and he needed to talk to her. He didn't know how to separate his personal feelings from the job she'd hired him to do.

Before he could muster the courage to knock, the door swung open, and there she stood. One hand on the door, the other on her hip. A meek smile across her lips. She was wearing sweatpants and a hoodie with a big beige stain on the front.

"Hi, Micah."

He pointed at the stain.

She didn't glance down at it. "Oatmeal."

"You haven't returned my texts," he said, trying to say it as a matter of fact, but it had probably come out as whiny and full of self-pity. He couldn't tell.

She ducked her head. "I know. I'm sorry. It's just that we... after the coffee shop."

Micah was about to respond when he heard a high-pitched sound, like the yip of a dog. He looked past Daisy to see a tiny person dressed in a one-piece flannel outfit. He was holding a laptop to his chest, barely able to hang on to the big gray rectangle.

"That's Caden," she said.

Caden crossed the living room, not really walking, but more of a lumbering stagger. Like a miniature drunk person.

"Mamamamama," Caden babbled.

Daisy grabbed Micah by the hand and pulled him inside.

"I don't want him to escape into the hallway," she said.

As the door shut behind him, Micah noticed a plastic sheath-like device on top of the knob, loosely hanging from it. This weird thing puzzled him for a moment. Some anti-kid device to make it hard for the toddler to grip the doorknob. He was fairly sure that hadn't been here last time.

"Caden, can you say hi to mommy's friend?"

Caden looked up at Micah towering over him, and grinned with a half-set of diminutive teeth. Then Caden ran right at Daisy's legs, wrapping his arms around her calves. The laptop tumbled onto the carpet.

"He's in a bit of a shy phase around strangers," Daisy said.

"I can relate," Micah said, and she smiled a little. "Look, Daisy, we need to talk. It's important."

She nodded gravely. "I understand. It's about time for a nap anyway. Can you help me?"

Micah had zero idea what to do with toddlers, but he shrugged and said, "lead the way."

Daisy picked up a sippy cup from the floor and shoved it in Caden's mouth. He tilted his head back and took a few gulps, then dropped the cup back on the floor. The cup tumbled around, leaking juice onto the carpet. Daisy didn't even notice.

She swept up the little human in her arms. Daisy groaned when she hoisted him up on her hip, but he looked like he couldn't weigh more than twenty pounds.

She jerked her head toward her bedroom, and Micah followed. She put Caden on a blanket on top of her dresser to change his diaper. She was like a ninja at it. Unzipped his outfit and swept it back. Ripped off his diaper in two quick motions, then lifted his butt a couple of inches off the dresser as she slid a fresh diaper underneath and had the new one fastened in about 0.2 seconds.

"That was impressive," Micah said.

She pointed behind him. "Will you get a binky from that jar over there?"

"A what?"

"Pacifier. He's down to only using them at naps, but he won't sleep without it."

Micah located a little pacifier in a glass jar on her

nightstand, and Caden started grunting as soon as he saw it in Micah's hand. Micah held it out and Caden opened his mouth. The binky filled the kid's mouth like plugging a hole. Caden met his eyes, and Micah's chest pulsed for a quick second. This baby was looking through him, staring at a generic grownup with no name and no identity other than *stranger*.

Micah hadn't interacted with a small child in so many years that he'd forgotten what it was like.

Daisy thanked him, and she rocked Caden in her arms for thirty seconds. Micah watched the little guy's eyes dim as the binky pulsed back and forth in his mouth.

She laid him in a crib next to her bed and held a finger to her lips as she ushered Micah out of the room and flicked off the light behind her.

"It's good to see you with him," Micah said as they returned to the living room. "You look happy when he's around."

She gave a wan smile. "Mama told me that you can't ever know what it's like to love someone else until you have a child of your own. That you won't understand sacrifice until you have to let go of something you want for your babies."

"I'll bet you're a great mom."

"I want to be one. I don't think I have been, though."

"How often do you get to see him?"

Her eyes instantly became wet. "Once every couple months."

"That's got to be tough."

"Last time I was with him, he could say only two or

three words. Now, it's like he can repeat almost anything I say back to him. It's beautiful and crazy and heartbreaking, all at the same time."

They sat on the couch and she ran her hands through her hair. "I'm sorry I didn't text you back. It's just that I have… complications with men sometimes, and what happened the other night…"

She trailed off, wiped a tear from her cheek. Micah placed his hand on top of hers. "It's okay, Daisy. Really, it's okay."

Her tears continued to fall and she pulled her hand back. This wasn't how this conversation was supposed to go.

Micah felt like he needed to say something. Give her something personal to distract her from this spiral of past guilt. He breathed in and out a few times, worked up the courage to say what he needed to say. Had he ever mentioned this to anyone besides Frank? He didn't think so, but maybe it was time to share the secret, to give it less power over him.

"I had this friend, a few years ago," Micah said. "His name was Pug. He was a good guy, you know? Loyal, fun, the kind of guy who would never let you down."

Daisy leaned over, gripped his hand, and said nothing. Kept her eyes on him.

"Pug passed away, and it was my fault. It was because of things that I did, or didn't do… I don't know how to explain it right. All I have left of him is a couple of pictures and a flash drive with some music he gave me. For a long time, I couldn't say his name out loud. I wouldn't let myself think it. But now that I've been sober for a while, I'm learning how to forgive myself for what happened. So I can move on."

Micah took a breath and had a hard time swallowing. He felt a little shaky, and Daisy must have sensed it. She held his hand tighter. He wondered why she was holding his hand now, since she'd shied away from his touch only a few seconds before.

"Sometimes," Micah said, "I'll go days without thinking about him at all. Then I'll be listening to music, and I hear a new song, and I think, 'oh, Pug would love this.' And then it's like the grief squeezes me, because I realize Pug will never hear that song. He can't."

"But you get to hear it."

Micah nodded, couldn't reply.

"I've lost people too," she said. "I lost my brother because of drugs. He got mixed up with the wrong people, and so he never had the chance that I have right now. I get so angry about it sometimes, but I can't do anything."

"That's the shitty part of being human, isn't it? You hurt people, or they hurt you, or they leave you unexpectedly and you don't have any answers or closure."

"Makes it hard to trust."

"Exactly."

"When's your birthday?" she said. "What month?"

"Sobriety birthday or belly-button birthday?"

"Your real birthday."

"May."

"Taurus. Okay, I can see that. Your people don't trust others easily."

"My people? You mean mostly-white guys from Oklahoma?"

She grinned and ducked her head. "Make fun if you want, but astrology isn't usually wrong about these things. It's about as close to a science as it can get."

Micah shrugged. "If you say so. But Daisy, when I said we needed to talk, I didn't come here to chat about the alignment of the stars or about what happened with us the other night. It's about Nathan."

She winced at him, and he felt conflicting pangs of longing and guilt. He was attracted to her, no doubt about that. But she was only a couple months sober and off drugs, and he knew how dangerous sex could be in those early stages of sobriety. He hadn't even considered that two nights ago.

He should have, though. Could have alleviated much of the awkwardness of this conversation.

"What's going on with Nathan?"

He debated telling her about the makeshift surgery clinic but didn't see the point. "It's almost over."

"What does that mean?"

"He and his buddies are going to meet somewhere out of town. So, for now, you're safe. And we're going to get them before they have a chance to come back into town. This will all be over by tomorrow night."

"You have a plan?"

"Well, no, not yet, I don't."

She didn't seem assured by his lack of details, and he didn't know what to say. He couldn't provide details he didn't have, and he knew better than to make sweeping promises about how no one would ever hurt her again. Daisy seemed too smart to believe in empty promises, anyway.

A plan sounded like a good idea. Now, he needed to get one of those.

# CHAPTER TWENTY-EIGHT

A LEC AUERBACH STOOD at the door to his private hangar near Denver International Airport. He could tell something was off immediately, even before typing in the code on the keypad. The plastic case covering the keypad was slightly angled, as if it had been removed and then replaced in a rush.

Could have been the wind that did that. Could have been a person.

Alec drew his pistol and keyed in the code, then leaned forward into the dark hangar. No one home.

"If you're in here, come out now and I'll kill you quickly. If you make me chase you, it's going to get a lot worse."

No reply.

Alec flicked the light switch, and the overhead lights ticked on one by one, like a row of dominoes. Humming softly.

He crept inside, keeping his pistol at a downward

angle so he wouldn't shoot anyone by accident. Alec only liked to shoot people on purpose. Accidental killings were always a big mess, especially if it was someone who worked for him and Nathan. Telling their families, paying them off... those scenarios always dragged on for endless amounts of time and became increasingly expensive.

Alec crossed the hangar, toward the office in the corner. The light was off, but that didn't mean no one was at home. When he reached the door, he tried it and found it locked. He jabbed in his key and yanked it back. Pistol up.

There was no one here, but Alec noticed right away that some of the papers on Nathan's desk weren't arranged properly. Alec always straightened any papers sitting around. Seemed unlikely that he might have left them to sit in a messy pile. Nathan would have, but Alec hardly ever allowed a mess to persist for too long.

He left the office and glanced around. He checked the collection of coolers next to the office. All of them were in uniform stacks, except for the third one from the top in the fourth row. It was slightly ajar. Someone had been looking in the coolers.

Alec fished his phone out and called Nathan, still keeping the gun in one hand.

"It's me," Alec said once Nathan had answered.

"Obviously," Nathan said.

"We need to talk."

"Seriously, Alec, I can't drive down to Georgetown again. I have way too much going on right now."

"I'm on a burner phone. We can talk freely. Listen to me, Nate. Is Z still in town?"

"No, he's up here with me. What's going on?"

Alec stowed his gun so he could check the desk drawers for missing items. "Someone's been in the hangar, but it's supposed to have been cleared out since Wednesday. Everything feels out of place here."

Nathan breathed on the other end for a second or two. "Anything important missing?"

"Not that I can tell. We haven't had any cargo here all week, so I'm not sure what they would have found."

"Maybe they weren't looking to take something. More like leave something behind."

Alec stood up straight. "You think our friends did this?"

"Could be. I haven't seen Welker at all today."

Alec sighed. That racist cop, the one who referred to Alec and Nathan as his *Polack associates.* He was something of a necessary evil.

Not for much longer, though. No more payoffs, no more limiting cargo shipments.

"Maybe he knows what's coming at the meet in Vail. He could have been poking around, trying to find our angle."

"No reason to assume that," Nathan said. "But no reason to trust him, either. What are you doing there? Why aren't you up here yet?"

"I'll be there tomorrow with plenty of time to spare. I came back to drop off a little present for your girlfriend yesterday."

Nathan hesitated. "Z and I had a long talk about her,

and he helped me to see I'm being too sentimental. If you need to take care of her, that's okay with me."

Alec considered it. "I think I can handle Daisy. I'm going to check in on her later, so we'll see."

"I'll leave it up to you."

Alec paused when an idea popped into his head. "That guy who was sniffing by the warehouse on Tuesday, the one who got into a fight with Z?"

"Yeah?"

"Did you get a look at his face?"

"No," Nathan said. "You think it's someone we know?"

"What about the guy you told me about? The neighbor, Micah Reed."

"Could be. It's entirely possible that if Reed is the same guy who was poking around the other day, he might have come back to break in."

"Makes sense," Nathan said. "Sounds like he may be more involved than I'm comfortable with."

"I'll stop by his apartment later when I visit Daisy. Give him a message too, maybe a stronger one than Daisy gets."

"Just do it clean, Alec. No mistakes."

He bit his lip and wondered if Nathan had said that out of thoroughness, or if it had been some passive-aggressive comment suggesting Alec was likely to make a mistake. Hard to tell from Nathan's tone of voice, sometimes.

"You there?" Nathan said.

Alec chose to ignore the previous comment. "You don't need to worry about me. I'll get rid of Reed and make sure Daisy understands to keep her mouth shut. If there's a communication problem, I'll take it further."

They said their goodbyes and Alec was about to close up the hangar when he noticed something along the back wall. An object sticking up from the floor. The pressure panel had been triggered, but someone had shoved a screwdriver in it to prevent it from activating the silent alarm.

He knelt next to it and tapped a finger on the handle sticking up into the air.

"Son of a bitch."

Nothing he could do about it now, so he deactivated the trap by disarming the security panel hidden in the nearby wall, then closed up the hangar.

He took the screwdriver with him, for good measure. Maybe he could get someone to pull a set of prints from it. Or maybe not. If he found any prints, they would most likely be from Micah Reed.

When he stepped outside, a blast of headlights blinded him. He lifted a hand to block out the light, then he squinted to identify the driver of the car.

Everett Welker.

Everett killed the lights and got out of the car. Big shit-eating grin as he hooked his thumbs into his belt loops and moseyed toward Alec.

Alec gripped the screwdriver in his hand.

"Hey, hey, little Auerbach brother, what's shaking?"

"I was leaving. What are you doing here?"

Everett took a comb from his back pocket and ran it through his thinning hair. "Came to log a delivery. Our guy is at the warehouse right now, and he'll be on his way here within the hour. I was going to meet him."

Alec narrowed his eyes. Everything this detective said was like an accusation. Alec reminded himself to breathe, that he only had to put up with Everett for a one more day, until Vail.

Once the meeting happened, all business would be finalized at the mid-mountain restaurant. No more kick-backs and payoffs to people who didn't deserve it. No more of Nathan and Alec sleeping with scorpions, always checking their flesh for stabs of deception.

Everett glanced down at the screwdriver in Alec's hand. Alec had to resist the urge to leap forward and drive it into Everett's neck.

*Not now, not yet. Be patient.*

Alec stepped aside, leaving Everett a clear path to the door. "Okay, then, Detective Welker. I won't get in your way."

# CHAPTER TWENTY-NINE

MICAH SAT AT the park across the street from the warehouse in Broomfield, waiting for the sun to set. He watched some kids swinging on the swing sets, but only for a minute. He didn't want to seem like some creeper, so he diverted his eyes to his phone when he felt like it had been going on for too long.

"Broomfield, huh?" said a deep voice behind him.

Micah swiveled on his bench seat to find Layne standing nearby, motorcycle helmet in hand. Despite the cold, he was still wearing only a muscle shirt and jeans. He was, however, holding a leather jacket in his other hand. Was supposed to snow tonight for the first time since April.

"Yep," Micah said. "Broomfield. You deliver Louis the bunny to your daughter?"

"Her birthday's next week. Louis is sitting comfortably

on my couch right now. Wanna tell me what we're doing here, man?"

Micah waved Layne to join him on the bench. "In a second. Your business out of town the other day go okay?"

Layne made a face. "I guess. I have to leave town again later tonight, but this is for work. That other thing was personal."

"Yeah, when you got that text the other day when we were at the warehouse… that was unexpected, wasn't it?"

Micah realized he might be fishing too hard to get Layne to explain himself. To clarify that weird look on his face when he'd gotten a message and had suddenly asked Micah to take him back to his motorcycle.

But Layne didn't seem affected by the probing. "Sure as shit was. That was my ex with another crisis that turned out to be nothing. It's not even worth going into all the gory details."

And Micah didn't know why, but he believed Layne. Maybe it was the way Layne seemed to let everything roll off his shoulders like water. Some kind of Harley-riding Zen master.

"Lemme tell you," Layne said, "don't get married, if you can help it. And if you do get married, don't have kids. And if you do have kids, don't get divorced. It can get to so many levels of ugly so fast. But if I knew then, know what I mean?"

"Afraid I don't. Never been married, no kids."

Layne winced. "Don't get me wrong. My daughter gives me all the reasons I need to get out of bed every morning. But her mom… that's a whole other story."

Micah couldn't even picture a messy divorce involving a child. That was so far out of his realm of experience, all he could do was shrug in response.

"Alright, man, time to fess up. What's going on here?"

Micah looked around the park, at the kids swinging not far from them. "Take a walk with me."

"Lead the way."

Micah headed away from the swings, along a bike path back into some trees, and Layne kept pace with him. They stumbled on a small pond on the other side of the trees, and they walked in a circle around the bank.

"Those coolers at the warehouse the other day?" Micah said.

"Yep?"

"That airport is a hub, but not for drugs. For human organs."

"Like stolen organs?"

"Exactly."

"You're kidding."

Micah shook his head.

"That's bat-shit crazy," Layne said, then sucked on his teeth for a moment. "You have proof of this?"

Micah pointed back through the trees at the warehouse complex behind them. "I can show you the room where they've been performing the surgeries."

"If you know who's involved and exactly where it's happening, why are we not here with a SWAT team?"

"You remember that cop I told you about who harassed me at the station up in Boulder? I saw him here, yesterday. The cops are in on it. I don't know how many of them, but it's enough that I'm not willing to call this in. Not even as an anonymous tip until I have proof I can use."

"You've been inside already."

"Yes."

Layne knelt and skipped a small pebble across the water. "Then if this is round two, I'd assume our goal here is to bust up the place?"

Micah nodded.

Layne grinned and slipped on his jacket. "Hell yeah, man. This is my kind of party."

# CHAPTER THIRTY

MICAH AND LAYNE stood outside the entrance to the smaller warehouse. Layne had his gigantic Peacemaker and a flashlight, Micah a crowbar. Micah wondered if he should have also had a gun, but dismissed the notion. They weren't here to kill everyone. At least, Micah wasn't here to kill everyone. He wasn't sure what Layne would do if they encountered resistance on the other side of this door.

The boards had been reattached outside. Micah pried them off.

"What's the square footage in there?" Layne said.

"The main room is about twenty by twenty. The back room, past the hidden door in the drywall, is about twenty feet wide, but it's fifty or sixty feet long. It's sectioned off by dividers, like hospital room curtains."

Layne looked skyward, nodding to himself. "Got it. I'll take high and to the right, you take low and to the left. We'll move through the room together. Sound good?"

"Sounds good. But, you don't have to do this, Layne. You can walk away now, if you want to."

Layne shook his head. "Not a chance. We started this, and now it's time to end it. I'm not a halfway-in kind of person. That work for you?"

"Works for me."

"Okay, man, eyes and ears open," Layne said.

Micah lowered his stance, and Layne opened the door into a dark room. He swung the flashlight around the find it in the same state as before. Tall shelves lined with boxes and crates. Pattern of footprints in the dust on the floor.

Except Micah could hear something coming from the back room behind the secret door in the drywall. Rectangular outline of light at the edges of the door, like white lines in the wall. He held up a finger to his lips and gestured at the wall with the crowbar. Layne pointed his flashlight at the floor near it and nodded.

Layne held up two fingers and made a swirling motion, then he pointed at himself, then Micah, then the back door.

Micah leaned in close and whispered, "Uh, I have no idea what your hand signals mean."

"Fair enough," Layne whispered back, grinning. "I'll open the door and go in first. Just like I said outside, I'll secure the right half of the room and you check on the left."

Micah nodded and waved the crowbar toward the door.

They crept along through the room, weapons ready.

Layne reached the door first, and Micah pointed to the divot in the drywall to use as finger holds.

Layne ripped it back and charged forward into the fully-lit room, but there was no one there. He pivoted right, raising his gun.

Then, from behind the door, a face came into view. The chubby cop from the other day, wearing civilian clothes. In his visible hand was a buzzing taser gun, which the cop jabbed into Layne's back.

Layne roared and stumbled forward. He slipped on the bloody tile, collapsing into one of the fabric room dividers. He took it with him to the ground as he fell. His body thunked onto the tile as the fabric folded around him like a net.

Micah jumped inside, swinging his crowbar at the cop's exposed hand. He knocked the stun gun free and smashed the cop's hand in the process. Micah heard the crack of bones as his attack connected.

The chubby cop yelped and gripped his hand, and then he tumbled back a step. He bumped against the wall. Held out his wrist, mewling in pain. But he recovered quickly and snatched at his gun with his good hand.

Micah swiped again, knocking the pistol free. It skittered across the floor, then clattered to a stop against the near wall. Lucky it didn't go off.

"You again," the cop said, sneering. "You're like a bad penny."

Micah didn't bother with a witty reply. He spun, trying to gather momentum and catch the cop off guard, but he was too slow. By the time he'd turned around, the cop had his flashlight out and ready to block Micah's crowbar. Metal clashed against metal.

The cop pulled the flashlight back toward himself, which Micah wasn't expecting. Micah had been pressing with all his weight, and the sudden change made him stumble forward. His feet slipped.

The cop used Micah's momentum to push the crowbar down and to the right, shifting Micah off balance. Then, the cop swung the flashlight at Micah's exposed shoulder. Pain like the stab of the knife shot down his arm.

The cop now jabbed at Micah's face, and Micah leaned back, out of range. He could hear stirring behind him. Layne getting to his feet.

Micah was off balance, so he wasn't quick enough to dodge the next blow, which came at his thigh. A burst of pain exploded up and down his left leg.

For a big guy, his adversary was surprisingly lithe and agile with that heavy flashlight in his hands. Micah was outmatched, and he knew it.

He stumbled, and the pain in his leg and shoulder had grown so intense he worried he might pass out. Head throbbed and his ears rang. He raised the crowbar, expecting an attack at his head, when the cop froze. Looked past Micah.

"Drop that damn flashlight," Layne said.

Micah peered around to see Layne on his feet, his .45 out and pointed at the cop's face.

The cop did as he was told and the flashlight clanked onto the tile floor. He raised his hands. The one Micah had hit with the crowbar was bent at a sickening angle. His face twisted into a portrait of rage, but he made no effort to flee or resist.

The cop had to know that in this small space, Layne was unlikely to miss, and that cannon of a gun could punch a hole big enough that he'd bleed out in a couple of minutes.

"On your knees," Layne said.

The cop dropped to his knees, and Layne stomped across the tile to him. Placed the gun against his temple.

"Don't," Micah said.

Both Layne and the cop paused, looked at Micah.

"Why not?" Layne said.

"He's a cop."

Layne pulled back the hammer of his Colt and kept his eyes on the officer. "He's a dirty cop, if he's into this organ trade shit."

Micah realized that because of the tile, if Layne did happen to miss, that bullet might ricochet several times. Any pull of a trigger in this little room was a dangerous proposition.

"Please, don't," Micah said. "Think about it. Killing him gets us nowhere."

Layne pulled the gun back an inch. "You have a better idea in mind?"

Micah removed four of his six zip ties from his back pocket, then changed his mind and got out the other two. He'd require all six of them to hog-tie this big boy.

Layne took a step back and waved Micah forward. Micah held up a finger and twirled it to make the cop to turn around. Tied the cop's hands together, then his feet.

"You think we've never been robbed before?" the cop said as Micah lowered him to the floor, resting his face against the tile. "You guys have no idea what you're doing. Kill me, don't kill me, it doesn't make any difference. You're both dead either way."

"Shut your stupid mouth," Layne said. "If I want your opinion, I'll ask for it."

Micah crouched in front of the cop. He took out his phone and snapped a few pictures of his face. The cop's eyes shot wide open and he tried to shield his face from the flash of the camera. Didn't matter. Micah already had a half dozen clear pictures of him.

"Got you that time," Micah said

"What do you people want?" the cop said.

"The freezer in the back. Tell me the combination, and I'll keep my friend here from shooting you in the face."

The cop smirked. "You said killing me gets you nowhere."

"Sure I did. But that doesn't mean I won't let him shoot you, if you don't tell me what I want to know."

The cop turned his pleading eyes to Layne, who cleared his throat and grinned down at him. "Don't look at me, man. I'm not the guy in charge here. I'm the hammer."

"Fine," the cop said. "But if I tell you this, you might as well go ahead and shoot me. They'll kill me anyway."

"That's your problem, not ours," Layne said.

The guy grudgingly spit out the combination to the freezer. Micah stumbled toward it, his body aching from the battle with the cop. He noted that the dead woman on the gurney was no longer there.

Layne guarded the cop as Micah typed on the keypad, then hefted the giant lid of the freezer. Cold steam escaped and crept over the edges of the freezer like fog rolling in from the ocean. Inside were smaller containers packed with ice.

Nestled among the ice chips were *organs*. Human organs.

Micah's stomach turned, and he might have puked if he didn't think Layne would judge him for it. So Micah swallowed back the bile and breathed deeply through his mouth to settle his nerves.

"You got maybe two hours left on those hearts," the cop said. "After that, they're just meat."

"Layne, do you know where the closest hospital is?"

"Uhh," Layne said, dragging out the word in a guttural sound. "We're in Broomfield? Good Samaritan is up 287. Maybe three miles from here."

"You're taking our product to a *hospital*?" the cop said, growling and wrestling against the zip ties. "Do you have any idea how much money you're throwing away?"

Micah walked back over to the cop, took out his phone, and dialed.

"911, what's your emergency?"

"My name is Roland Templeton. I've made a citizen's arrest on a police officer who's been dealing in stolen human organs. I need you to come pick him up, right away."

# PART III

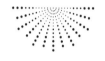

## HERE BE BLOOD THIEVES

# CHAPTER THIRTY-ONE

FRANK BREATHED IN the crisp night air in Vail, a half hour further west from Frisco. The little town, dripped into a crack between the mountains, was supposed to be like a European village. Quaint shops with spaces for rent above them made up the shopping areas, with cobblestone and brick streets that curved all around the town. But the ultra-modern multi-million dollar condos didn't quite jibe with this throwback Swiss chalet vision. Local PD drove luxury cars.

Frank didn't care one way or another. He hardly ever made it up into the mountains, so Vail could do whatever the hell they wanted with their town.

The snow on the runs looked patchy and thin, not quite ready for ski season. Not that Frank would slap on a pair of those uncomfortable boots and the goggles and engage in that whole mess. Not just for the fact that his knees wouldn't tolerate all that bending, but he was pretty sure he'd end up wrapped around a tree his first time down the slopes.

He left his car in the main tourist parking lot structure and ventured into the village. He strolled by the condo building named Mountain Haus, toward the covered bridge, and then out into the tourist areas. White buildings with deeply stained wooden accents. Antique placards with the names of restaurants swung from hooks out in front. T-shirt shops, ice cream parlors, homemade fudge, upscale art galleries.

Hundreds of people milled about from shop to bar, bundled up in trendy winter coats and hats. Frank was surprised; he didn't think there'd be much to do here in pre-ski season, but that didn't seem to keep the people away.

Frank wasn't sure where to begin with his investigation. Micah's translation of Nathan and Zaluski's conversation had suggested a deal going down or some other kind of big meeting in town, tomorrow night. Hell, maybe it was a summit of all the organ traffickers in the tri-state area.

So Frank was keeping an eye out for something unusual, but he didn't know what. A meeting place, or some clue as to what was going to happen. He'd tried to follow Nathan and Zaluski earlier in Frisco, but they'd split up and Frank had lost track of them. No sign of Detective Everett Welker, either.

Who were they meeting, and for what purpose? Were they expanding their territory, bringing in a new distributor, or possibly negotiating some trade deal? Having these bits of information would help, but Frank had no idea where to begin with that.

He was going into this blind, and that made his stomach queasy. First rule of an investigation was to invent a way to get the upper hand, and hold onto it tightly.

Finding Nathan's Aston Martin or Zaluski's Mercedes would be a good place to start, but there were no cars to be found driving around. Like the quaint village the town was trying to be, most of the streets were pedestrian only. Cars usually parked back at the covered four-story structure off I-70.

And then, Frank felt like an idiot for not checking the structure before he left. He hoofed it back over the covered bridge and across the brick courtyard in front of Mountain Haus, and then into the structure. He paused inside the parking garage, winded. He wasn't at a much higher altitude than Frisco, but damn, he had zero energy here.

He checked the first floor, second floor, and when he was on the third floor, he spotted that gray Mercedes Zaluski had been driving the last couple days.

Frank approached cautiously, hand on the gun in his hip holster. The car looked empty, but he wasn't taking any chances. He paused, squinting at the tinted windows to spot any movement.

So, Zaluski was here, and that meant Nathan was here, and probably his brother Alec and Detective Everett Welker. And, whoever they were meeting.

Unless Nathan was meeting with Everett. That would

make sense; cops and robbers having a summit to work out their differences.

When Frank was satisfied that the car was empty, he lifted his hand off the pistol and walked normally to the car. Checked the back seat, nothing. But when he crossed the front, he noticed a tiny slip of paper on the dashboard.

A parking permit for Mountain Haus.

"Hello, Mr. Zaluski," Frank said to the windshield. "Not so hidden now, are you?"

# CHAPTER THIRTY-TWO

WHEN DAISY EXITED the elevator onto Micah's floor, her heart leaped into her throat. But she had to do this. She had to tell Micah the truth about why she'd so impulsively slept with him two days ago, and why she'd been so distant after. She owed him the whole story, but not only for him. She owed it to herself.

Part of this new life free of drugs and alcohol was to be brutally honest, no matter how uncomfortable it felt. She hadn't been honest with him. And it was eating at her, making her crave the escape of a pill or a drink or a line.

But a small, selfish part of her longed for company. Since saying goodbye to Caden two hours ago, her heart had ached. The apartment had once again become a husk of a thing. A place to sleep and eat and watch television, but not a home.

Micah would make her feel better. Take her mind off the loneliness.

And she knew how ironic it was that she was looking to *Micah* for reassurance. She closed her eyes, drew in a deep breath, and readied herself to approach his front door.

But something strange happened when she opened her eyes.

The door was wide open.

She tiptoed across the carpet and peered inside his door. The coffee table was overturned, shattered glass sprinkled on the carpet like breadcrumbs. His television was sitting on his couch, the LCD screen in pieces.

She clutched the crucifix on her necklace and rubbed her thumb and forefinger across it. Asked Jesus to help her keep calm.

Daisy leaned in and spied the kitchen. The fridge was open and all of his food was strewn about the floor, like the aftermath of a food fight. There were holes in the wall in the small dining room area, and his dining table had been broken in two.

Such chaos, as if a pack of wild horses had trampled through here. Micah had nice stuff. The television alone had to be worth a thousand dollars.

Normally, given the chance, she might feel the desire to snoop and find out what other nice things he had. But not now. All she could think was that Nathan had to have done this, and if that were true, then he knew that Daisy had gone to Micah for help. That meant a death sentence for both her and Micah.

Nathan had warned her to stay away, to keep her head down and not talk to anyone. She still wore the fading remnant of a black eye as a reminder of his demands. And she'd disobeyed him, so he would feel justified in punishing her.

*Flee. Get out of here.*

She spun and launched toward the elevator, but she stopped short. At the end of the hall near her escape route stood Alec, his brown eyes flared.

"Hi there. You don't live on this floor."

She gulped. "No."

"That's interesting," Alec said, putting a hand on his chin and rubbing it in a show of exaggerated confusion. "I wonder what you're doing up here. Can you explain it to me?"

"Alec, please."

He bared his teeth and stomped across the carpet toward her. In his rage, he looked exactly like his brother. The same evil written all over his face.

He snatched her by the arm and yanked her toward the elevator. "Please *what*, Daisy? Do you think, after all the trouble you've caused, that you get to make demands of me?"

"I didn't do anything!"

Alec pointed at Micah's door. "The guy you're here to see? Did you know he broke into my hangar? Stole important documents that belong to me and Nathan?"

"I don't know anything about that," she said, "and I don't see what it has to do with me. There's nothing going on here."

Alec wasn't listening. He shoved her into the elevator and stomped inside after her. In a flash of motion, he jabbed the button for her floor and then faced her, shoulders pumping as he breathed. Pure anger. He looked like the devil, nostrils flared, eyes wide, eyebrows like a V on his forehead.

Daisy knew that at any second, he was going to wrap his hands around her throat and choke her. She wouldn't be able to stop him. She didn't have a gun, or pepper spray, or anything else to defend herself. She couldn't keep him away.

The elevator pinged and the door opened. He stepped out of the way and waved a hand. "Go."

For a moment, she stood frozen, confused. He wasn't going to kill her? Alec looked down at her, the V of his eyebrows slowly reverting back to flat as he seemed to calm down.

Something inside her clicked, and she realized she could walk away and he would stay in the elevator. She was safe, in a manner of speaking.

She said nothing, only pulled her purse close to her chest and slipped past him. Turned to face him one last time as the elevator doors whooshed.

"Bye, Daisy."

The doors shut. An internal debate raged inside her head for a few seconds, but she decided she needed to tell him about this. She whipped out her phone and composed a text.

*Micah, please hurry back here. Alec was in your apartment. He trashed everything.*

# CHAPTER THIRTY-THREE

MICAH AND LAYNE rolled up to the emergency room entrance of the Good Samaritan hospital, popped the trunk, and hopped out of the car. Micah left it running. They yanked the living hearts from the containers nestled in the trunk, as many as they could, as quickly as they could.

Micah watched for security or someone else to come running out, but nothing happened. No one seemed to care that they were unloading coolers full of *whatever* on the front steps of the emergency room.

*Don't mind us. Just dropping off some hearts.*

When they'd unloaded the last one, Micah made eye contact with someone in scrubs inside and waved his arms to get the woman's attention.

She cocked her head at him and he beckoned her outside. He didn't wait for her. Security and then the police might be more than a little interested to know what they were doing with human organs in the trunk of a Honda Accord.

Explaining everything to the police? That could come later.

Micah whistled at Layne and they jumped in the car. That's when Micah's phone buzzed. As they peeled out of the parking lot, he wrenched it free from his pocket and read the text from Daisy.

"Bad news?" Layne said.

"Do you mind if we go downtown before I take you back to your bike?"

Layne blew out some air. "Yeah, I guess that's okay, if we hurry, man. I do need to be on the road up to Cheyenne before too long. Is this detour serious?"

"These guys we messed with, they busted up my apartment."

"How could that be? We left there ten minutes ago."

"No, I think they've known about me for a few days. Our friend the cop must have tipped them off after I went to the police station. Seems like they're now getting around to sending me a message."

"Sons of bitches," Layne said, and left it at that.

Instead of turning back toward the warehouse, Micah hopped on Highway 36 to drive down to Denver. They rode in silence, which was not unusual. Micah liked that Layne didn't say anything if he didn't have anything to say. Micah had never cared much for small talk, anyway.

Instead, Layne stripped his .45 and cleaned it with a kit he took from his jacket. He barely even looked at the gun as he proceeded through the steps.

As they exited onto Speer and neared the condo, Micah said, "I appreciate everything you've done to help over the last couple days. I know it's a big leap of faith to do what we did back there."

Layne pushed out his lower lip, nodded like he was bobbing his head to music. "No sweat, man. You're an alright guy, and what those people are doing is some of the most messed up stuff I've ever seen. I hope you pull down their whole operation."

Micah wasn't sure if that was even his goal. What had started as a request for a damsel in distress to help her boyfriend had morphed into an ugly slide into police corruption, human organ trafficking, and who-knew-what else.

"I'm going to do what I can. I need to survive the next twenty-four hours, but I've been in worse spots before."

Micah parked in the below-ground garage and they hurried to the elevator. Layne loaded his .45 and Micah checked the battery on his newest toy, the pistol-grip taser with laser sighting he'd appropriated from the hog-tied cop back at the warehouse. Yes, he had stolen police property, but he didn't think that cop would come looking for it anytime soon. Hopefully, he was cuffed in the back of a police car now, while forensic specialists were combing over that sickening makeshift surgery room in Broomfield.

The thought occurred to Micah that the warehouse would probably link back to Nathan and Alec. So, if he did nothing else, there a good chance that those two would be implicated and face charges.

Or, they might skip town and escape capture. They obviously had access to a private hangar, so it wouldn't be unreasonable to think the Auerbach brothers might hop on a small plane to Venezuela.

And if they were forced to do that, they might have Daisy killed out of spite as a parting gift.

No, Micah couldn't take the path of least resistance. He had to solve the Nathan problem while he could, while there was still time. He had a perfect window where he knew exactly where both the brothers were going to be. Tomorrow night, in Vail.

As they rode the elevator to Micah's condo, he unlocked his phone to text Daisy, then he hesitated. Instead, he punched her floor button and the elevator halted on her floor.

"Gotta make a quick stop first," Micah said.

Layne shrugged as the door opened, and Micah emerged from the elevator. Layne stepped out but didn't follow, stood legs spread and arms crossed behind him, like a soldier at ease.

Micah strolled across the carpet. Didn't know why, but he felt the pressure of anxiety bear down on him, all at once. Like a weight settling on his shoulders.

He knocked on Daisy's door. His heart raced and he had trouble swallowing. "It's me."

In a moment, she opened the door, tears streaming down her face.

"You okay?" he said.

"Not really. Have you been to your condo yet? Maybe

you should bring the police with you. I didn't want to call them without asking you first."

"Don't worry about me. You don't know this about me, but I've been in these situations before. Plus, I brought a friend with me."

Micah pointed back at Layne, and Daisy leaned out to look. Layne gave a flip of the hand as a wave, and Daisy tried to smile, but it came out flat and uninspired.

Micah put a hand on her forearm. She glanced down at his touch but didn't shy away. Her skin was warm and soft, and he wanted to hug her but knew he couldn't.

"Listen to me. This is all going to be over by tomorrow night, so I need you to leave your apartment. Go stay with that friend you were talking about when we first met. Or a motel, or something. But don't be here or anywhere they can find you for the next twenty-four hours. This is really important, Daisy. Can you do that for me?"

She nodded, wincing back tears.

"This is all going to be okay. I'm going to end this."

# CHAPTER THIRTY-FOUR

"**S**HE'S CUTE," LAYNE said as the elevator doors opened.

"It's not like that."

"If you say so, man."

They approached Micah's condo carefully, foot over foot. The door was shut, and they each took one side. Weapons out.

Micah thought about all of his possessions inside. Daisy had said the apartment was trashed. His furniture, he didn't care much about. He had a nice TV he hardly ever watched, but his guitar collection was another matter. If that was destroyed, might make him break down in tears.

Micah met Layne's eyes and Layne nodded.

Micah pushed open the unlocked door to find his whole apartment in shambles. Tables turned over and broken, the single framed art print he'd had in his living room torn in two, his TV cracked, sitting on the couch.

Seeing his apartment in this state was more upsetting than he'd thought it would be. He wanted to whine for a moment about how he didn't have the cash to replace all this stuff, but he reminded himself that the mourning could come later. It was just stuff, anyway.

Now, he needed to make sure Alec hadn't left behind any booby traps or other surprises.

The shoebox.

Micah hitched in a breath when he thought of the shoebox hidden underneath the floorboards in his bedroom. The last remnants of his life as Michael McBriar, a few photographs and love letters from the girls who'd known him as a different person.

Objects that proved who he used to be.

The shoebox was filled with forbidden things he'd had to sneak with him after he'd moved to Denver, most of it harmless bits of nostalgia. Except for the white business card with the image of the wolf's head. That wasn't harmless at all, and no way could Micah explain that one to Layne.

Micah pointed at his chest and then pointed down the hall to the master bedroom. Layne grunted and wandered into the kitchen, gun drawn and ready. Micah hoped Layne wouldn't shoot him on the way back out.

As Micah crept down the hall, he cast a look into the smaller bedroom, a room mainly to function as storage for his guitars. He wanted to sink to his knees when he saw three of his guitars with broken necks, strings flayed and jutting out like mad scientist hair. Such a waste.

At least Alec hadn't touched his Ovation, that beautiful

electric-acoustic with the pristine green finish. While that ax wasn't priceless, it sure felt that way to Micah. Maybe Alec knew about guitars and couldn't bring himself to destroy such a work of art.

Micah cleared his head and pressed on, into the master bedroom. At first glance, it appeared untouched. Then, Micah noticed the pillows on his bed had been rearranged. Alec had come in here and sat down. Thinking that, Micah let a little shiver run down his spine.

But the carpet near the closet, where he could access the space under the floorboards, looked untouched. Micah peered back into the hallway—couldn't let Layne see this —and he lifted the carpet and peeled back one floorboard to check.

His shoulders slumped in relief. The shoebox was still there.

With another glance back in the hallway to check for Layne, Micah replaced the floorboard and reseated the carpet. Removing the shoebox to root around inside it wasn't a good idea. No way he'd take the chance of Layne interrupting that activity.

"All clear back here," he said.

"Nothing strange in the kitchen or living room," Layne said.

Micah left the room, now finally lowering the taser.

He met Layne in the hallway, next to the bathroom door. Layne stuck his pistol in the back of his waistband.

"Is anything missing?" Layne said.

Micah's laptop was in his car, his phone still in his

pocket. He didn't have much else of value that hadn't already been destroyed. "I don't think so."

"This doesn't make sense, man," Layne said, then he opened his mouth to continue, but the bathroom door burst open and a tall man leaped out, knife first. Teeth bared, a blur of flesh and clothing.

The knife drove straight at Layne, who managed to swipe his arm up to block the blow. The knife grazed off his shoulder, and Micah saw a trail of blood sail through the air as Layne tried to pull back.

The attacker was Nathan, or maybe Alec. Probably Alec, since that's who Daisy said had been on the floor.

Micah saw his chance, lifted the taser. He pointed it at Alec's side and squeezed the trigger, but nothing happened. In the meantime, Layne and Alec scrambled for the knife, Layne's hands wrapped around Alec's.

Micah didn't know if the taser's safety was on, or if the battery was drained, and it didn't matter. No time to check.

Had to act. Had to take advantage. Alec was occupied struggling with Layne.

Micah pressed his fingers together and jabbed Alec in the kidney, with all the force he could muster. His blow landed underneath Alec's rib cage.

Alec bent to the side, grimacing. One of his hands slipped off the knife, and Layne had almost stolen it away from him.

Micah reared back, made a fist, and jabbed Alec as hard as he could in the gut. Threw his hip into it. He followed with another punch to Alec's lower back.

Alec leaned forward from the blow, and Layne ripped the knife away. With his free hand, he jabbed Alec in the gut three or four times so quickly that his arm seemed to blur.

Alec stumbled back from the ferocity of the attack.

Layne got a hand around Alec's throat, pushed him against the wall next to the bathroom door. Alec was big, but Layne was bigger. He pressed up, lifting Alec off the carpet a full inch. Before Micah could do anything, Layne shoved the blade into Alec's chest, all the way to the hilt.

Alec heaved in a ragged breath as his mouth dropped open. His head jittered back and forth, and his eyes darted around the room. Disbelief on his face. He hadn't expected to die here tonight. He'd expected to kill the two people who'd infiltrated his private hangar by the airport.

That was the assumption, anyway. Not likely that Nathan and Alec already knew about the warehouse robbery.

Layne pushed Alec into the bathroom as the dying man feebly tried to swat at Layne's hands. He left bloody swipes on Layne's wrists, but couldn't grasp the hands to get at the knife.

Layne twisted the knife, Alec yelped, and Layne yanked out the blade.

A spurt of blood followed it. Alec bounced off the counter and slid to the tile. He looked down at the reddened hole in his chest, then back up at Micah.

Terror on his face.

"It's not…" he said, then his breathing seized and he coughed blood. He pressed his hands against the floor, trying to rise to his feet, but only managed to lift himself a couple inches before he fell back down, dazed.

He hitched a few breaths and then stilled.

"Son of a bitch," Layne said, chest heaving. "I don't even know how that happened. You okay?"

"Your shoulder," Micah said, pointing at the bloody gash in Layne's jacket.

Layne angled his head and frowned at the blood. "Shit. I don't know how he surprised us like that. I thought you'd already checked the bathroom."

Micah tried to ignore the jolt of guilt that Layne's injury was his fault. "We need to get you to a hospital."

Layne stripped off his jacket and examined the wound. "No hospital."

Micah thought about making a joke about how Layne's love of muscle shirts meant he'd only ruined the jacket, but he couldn't get the words out. Instead, he said, "what do you mean, no hospital? That's a deep cut."

Layne checked his watch. "Duct tape and a bandage will be fine. I have to be on my way to Cheyenne in less than two hours. I cannot be late. You gotta trust me, Micah, this has to happen. You want to call the cops, or you want to handle this ourselves?"

Micah looked at the corpse of Alec Auerbach, bleeding all over his bathroom tile. Cops meant an investigation, probably an order not to leave town. Micah needed to be on the road to Vail in the morning to meet Frank. He had to be there, with Frank, when the meeting happened tomorrow night.

Plus, who knew what kind of cops would show up to

answer the 911 call. The good ones, or the bad ones? Micah couldn't tell them apart.

"We handle it ourselves."

"Let's get a move on, then," Layne said. "I don't have any time to waste."

∾

## INSIDE WITSEC BLOG
## POST DATED 10.18

*First of all, I want to thank all of you for the comments and emails you've been sending to me. It's meant a lot to me to see this little blog get all this traction and get so many shares. It's not easy to write this. I know there's a chance someone could find me and cause me harm, even though all I'm trying to do is expose the truth.*

*But I feel like what I'm doing has to be done. This information needs to get out, because without it, all of us are less safe.*

*Now, on to business.*

*Today's post is about Phil Criselli. Phil worked as a driver for some gangsters in New York, in the Albany area. These gangsters didn't have a traditional mob "family" kind of business. They were from all over: New York, Canada, Michigan. Seemingly unrelated people. That's part of what made their organization so hard to bring down.*

*Now, about Phil, you might be thinking: just a driver? What's so terrible about that?*

*But what Phil did wasn't only drive people around. He helped his mob bosses cut up bodies and feed them into wood chippers, and he also helped his bosses find their kidnapping victims by scoping out politician's children at their schools. In his spare time, he extorted hard-working local businessmen out of their money.*

Just a driver, sure. But that's what he told them when he was arrested for kidnapping a state senator's daughter.

Phil joined WitSec after rolling over on his bosses and sending most of them to prison. He testified about knowledge of the planned kidnappings of more than six dozen children for ransom, the murder of a half dozen politicians who passed laws his bosses didn't like.

Phil spent a decade in prison for his kidnapping charge, as a reduced sentence for cooperation. He should have spent the rest of his life in prison.

When he became Todd Lancaster and moved to Dallas, nobody who lived around him knew anything about his brutal and devious past. And, what WitSec didn't know was that Todd started running an illegal sports betting pool out of the body shop where he worked. He eventually was arrested and spent a year in prison (as Todd Lancaster), but he's out now, running free in Texas. He's since left the Dallas area and I've been unable to track him down. But he's out there, this murderer and kidnapper, free to do it again, if he chooses. Because that's the American way. Freedom to hurt good citizens, if you do one little good thing and snitch on bad people, because then it means you're not a bad person anymore. Can you feel the sarcasm in my words?

Next post: a truly detestable person named Michael McBriar, who sold drugs and hurt people while he worked as a "driver" for the ruthless Sinaloa cartel.

# CHAPTER THIRTY-FIVE

∼

MICAH STARED OUT the window of Starbucks, watching Union Station across the street. The morning sun colored the building, lightening the beige stone.

Last night, he'd slept fifteen feet away from where he and Layne had killed Alec Auerbach. Actually, Layne had done the deed, but Micah had stood there and watched it happen. He'd been a part of it.

This wasn't the first time Micah had seen someone bleed to death in front of him. It wasn't even the first time Micah had been involved in the killing of a person. But, since entering Witness Protection, he had never taken a life without good reason, whether to protect someone or stop someone bad.

Alec was certainly a bad person. No, Alec's death bothered Micah for a different reason. It was the first time since changing his name and moving to Denver that Micah had brought violence home with him.

Something he'd hoped he would never have to do again. He didn't want to perpetuate violence of any kind. He had enough reminders of that whenever he moved his arms or legs, after the bruising that asshole cop had given him last night.

He took the severed head of Boba Fett and set him on the table in front of him. Boba didn't like spending all his time cooped up in Micah's pockets.

"Been a rough week, Boba."

Boba Fett stared back at him. The little piece of plastic was incapable of nodding sympathetically, but Micah believed it would if it could.

Micah's phone buzzed, and he checked it to see that he had a new email. He glanced at the email subject, a notification of a new blog post at the *Inside WitSec* blog. Time was short, he'd have to read it later. As soon as he finished this coffee, he was going to hit the road to Vail, to meet Frank. He'd wasted too much time already finding a charger that would fit his new taser gun, and then waiting for it to fully juice.

Micah hadn't spoken to Layne after he'd left last night. He and Layne had finished up their business mostly in silence, and Micah had rushed him back to his Harley so he could get on the road. To whatever strange business he had to attend to up in Cheyenne. This big secret business meeting he wouldn't talk about besides spitting vague phrases about how important it was.

Layne was an odd man, sometimes. Secretive, private.

Micah smiled down at Boba Fett's head, because he'd only known Layne for three or four days. Layne had a right to his privacy, and Micah had no idea what was normal for him. Or anyone, really.

Layne had saved his ass a couple times now, so there was no reason to doubt the guy. Plus, Layne wasn't any weirder than the kind of person who would talk to a Star Wars action figure in the middle of a populated coffee shop.

Micah drained the last of his coffee and tossed the empty into the trash can. As he stood, he spied a familiar face across the street, paying for a magazine at a news kiosk in front of Union Station.

Gavin Belmont, US Marshal.

Micah narrowed his eyes, slid on his coat, and left Starbucks. He barely checked at the crosswalk to see if any cars were coming, then made a straight line to Gavin, once he was on the Union Station side of the street.

"Gavin," Micah said.

Gavin stopped short and lifted his magazine in greeting. "Good morning. I was coming to see you, actually. Thought I'd catch you before you left for work this morning."

Micah thought about his condo, cleaned of Alec's blood and fingerprints. Had he and Layne been thorough? Would it stand up to Gavin's—or anyone else's—scrutiny? They'd doused the body with bleach before dumping it near the warehouse, hoping to send a message to the dirty cops. But there was no guarantee they hadn't missed something.

"I'm not going to work today," Micah said.

Gavin raised an eyebrow. "Oh? Why not? Have you reconsidered my offer?"

Micah eased closer, within a foot of the Marshal. "No, I haven't. I'm staying in Denver."

"I'm not going to wait around for you to pick a side, Micah."

"Listen to me. You want to do some good? Then this is what you're going to do."

Gavin smirked. "I'm all ears."

"There are some dirty cops in this town. They're in league with Nathan and Alec Auerbach, and Tomás Zaluski. They've been working the illegal organ trade."

Gavin's smirk leveled. "Okay, go on."

"Sounds like you've heard about this."

"There's been an ongoing investigation by the FBI, but I don't know much about it. Just bits and pieces I've heard in passing."

"Something is going down tonight in Vail. You and your Marshal buddies, or the FBI, or I-don't-care-who, need to get off your asses and arrest these people. One of them is a fugitive, so that should put it in your jurisdiction, right?"

"Is he a federal fugitive?"

Micah shrugged. "I'm not sure."

Gavin frowned. "I can't pull together some big task force within a day. It's not possible. I need proof, Micah, and I need time."

Micah held out his phone, flipping through the pictures he'd taken at the makeshift surgery room in the warehouse. Only now did he realize he'd been too distracted at the time to snap a picture of the dead woman on the gurney.

Micah stopped scrolling when he found the picture of the chubby cop. "I don't know this cop's name, but his badge number is 402. He was at the warehouse and he pulled a gun on me. He was arrested last night. Can you find out if he's weaseled out of it?"

"How did you get those pictures?"

Micah slipped his phone back into his pocket. "That's my business. Your business is to stop these people. Understand?"

Gavin turned up his palms. "I can see you're upset about this and you want to turn the world upside down, but I need more information. I need time to put something together. Why don't you come with me to the FBI's field office here and we can set up a meeting with some agents?"

"I don't have time."

Gavin pursed his lips, beginning to show his anger. "Then what do you expect me to do?"

"Come to Vail. Today."

Gavin bared his teeth. "I don't know who you think you're talking to. You don't give me orders."

"One more thing. There's a woman who lives in my building named Daisy Cortez. She needs help getting shared custody of her son. You can make that happen."

Now Gavin actually laughed. "Anything else? Need me to pick you up some Powerball tickets?"

Micah stared down Gavin for a moment, then he

turned and walked away. Gavin was going to help or he wasn't. Micah had no control over it.

"Come back here," Gavin said. "I need to know where you got those pictures, Micah. We're not done here."

Micah kept walking, but Gavin didn't follow him. That meant the Marshal believed him, or at least a little part of him did. Micah had to hope it would be enough.

# CHAPTER THIRTY-SIX

W HEN MICAH SAW Frank standing across the public parking garage in Vail Village, he had to resist the urge to wrap his arms around the old man. Not that Frank had ever seemed opposed to human contact, but Micah worried he might accidentally squeeze his boss to death.

Frank grinned and stuck out a hand. Micah hugged him anyway.

"Good to see you too, kid."

Micah pulled back. "Frank, so much has happened this week. I don't even know where to start."

"How about we get some lunch and you tell me all about it."

Micah agreed and they left the parking garage. The crisp cool of the air stung Micah's face as they strolled toward the village shops. He'd only been to Vail a couple times since moving to Colorado, but it had quite the upscale feeling, compared to the other ski towns. So clean, so organized. Everything had a place.

"Want to give me the high points?" Frank said as they crossed the covered bridge next to Mountain Haus.

Micah didn't know where to begin. Telling him about infiltrating the airplane hangar, the warehouse, meeting Layne, stealing those live human hearts, his conversations with Gavin Belmont, being attacked by Alec in the middle of his ruined apartment.

"I made a friend this week," Micah said.

"Good," Frank said. He pointed at the stone exterior of The Chophouse. "You up for a steak?"

"Of course, boss. I'm always up for a steak."

Frank let Micah climb the restaurant steps first, and Micah held the door open for the old man. Micah peered inside, making sure Nathan and Zaluski weren't lurking nearby. Micah's black eye had faded after their skirmish at the hangar, but he was certain the European would recognize him right away.

Micah paused, leaned close to Frank. "Do you have a plan?"

"Not really," Frank said, chewing on his lower lip. "Not a good one, anyway. We'll have to work that out, but we still have a few hours until dark."

Micah gave the hostess their names and they had a seat in the lobby to wait for a table.

"The girlfriend doing okay?" Frank said. "What was her name?"

"Daisy. She's still alive, which is one for the *plus*

column. Scared to death, but I asked her to hide out until this is all over."

Frank eyed him for a second, and Micah felt like Frank could see right through him. He shouldn't have slept with Daisy, obviously. But as far as he knew, there wasn't some kind of skip tracer/bounty hunter code of conduct about these things. Daisy's case wasn't even one officially sanctioned by Mueller Bail Enforcement.

But the bigger issue was that Micah was a year sober and Daisy was only sixty-something days sober. That's why Micah should have known better. Since Frank was his sponsor, Micah knew he'd have to tell the old man at some point. But maybe not today.

"Good," Frank said. "One less thing to worry about."

Micah leaned close to Frank and whispered in his ear. "Alec is dead. He broke into my apartment and attacked us, so we killed him last night."

"We?"

"That friend I told you about. Layne."

Frank shook his head. "You shouldn't involve other people in this business, Micah. It's not safe."

"Layne is okay. I trust him."

Frank stuck his thumb in his mouth and chewed on the nail. "Maybe you shouldn't. Lot of sharks out there, kid."

The hostess escorted them to a back table. Frank left first and Micah followed, now feeling his pulse speed up. Had trusting Layne been a terrible mistake?

Right now, that didn't matter. The meeting tonight was the only important thing on the agenda. Either they were going to interrupt this get-together and sabotage Nathan's criminal enterprise, or they were going to wind up dead. Didn't seem to be much middle ground.

∾

Mountain Haus, a Vail mainstay for decades, had two large conference rooms and two smaller meeting rooms. The smaller rooms were glorified walk-in closets with conference tables. And that didn't matter. Nathan had been fine with reserving a meeting room, until he learned that the smaller rooms were in the condo complex's basement. That would not do. He didn't expect anything to go wrong tonight, but if it did, there was no sense in being trapped with no escape route.

So they'd reserved a large conference room, despite the fact they were going to be few in number. Nathan, Alec, and Zaluski were meeting with Everett Welker and two of his associates who were looking to get into the game.

At least, that's what Everett and his cop buddies thought they were doing here. To negotiate fees for distribution and payoffs. But they didn't know the surprise in store for them.

Nathan stared at the glossy oak conference table, running his hands along it, telling himself that he felt confident. Project it, then eventually, he would feel it. He needed to be calm to convince Everett and the others to follow him up the mountain to the real meeting spot.

Meanwhile, Zaluski paced the outside of the room like a bomb primed to explode. He removed a machete from a leather scabbard inside his coat. He swung it a few times in the air, like a batter warming up.

"Where is Alec?" Zaluski said. "Have you heard from him?"

"He hasn't been returning my texts."

"This is a problem. This is a big problem."

"Maybe he went on a run."

Zaluski sighed through clenched teeth and re-sheathed his machete. "You think he went to Mexico now? On this day we've been planning for months?"

"He's done stuff like this before. I'm sure he'll get back to me in the next couple hours."

Zaluski took out a small glass device, about the size and shape of a tube of lipstick. He pressed it to his nose and jerked his head back.

"You need to lay off that shit," Nathan said. "It's not helping. If Welker and those guys show up here and you can't stop gritting your teeth, they'll think something's wrong."

Zaluski ignored him. "What if they already know? What if they got to Alec and pulled the information out of him?"

"Even if they knew, and even if they somehow detained Alec, he would never tell them anything. It's pointless to worry. Maybe you should sit down so we can talk about the plan for this evening."

Zaluski jerked a rolling chair across the carpet, sat for two or three beats, then jumped back up. Resumed his pacing.

Nathan sighed. But, at least as amped as Zaluski was,

Nathan felt like a milkshake in a snowstorm comparatively. Maybe he could do all the talking and send Z ahead up the mountain early.

No, if Nathan was here alone, that might look suspicious. They had to walk into the restaurant together, so it wouldn't seem staged. They'd arranged to have a private meeting space at The 10th, a restaurant off the Gondola One route up the mountain.

Where the hell was Alec? Nathan didn't think he had actually hopped on a plane for an unscheduled delivery to Mexico or Canada, but it could have been a girl. Alec had been known to wander into a bar and disappear with some piece of ass for a day or two. And it wouldn't be too unusual for Alec to do it at a goddamn critical time like today.

As much as Alec liked order and structure, he wasn't immune to pussy.

"I don't like this," Zaluski said.

"Worrying gets us nowhere. Can we just focus?"

Zaluski ripped another bump of coke. "No. I do not like this meeting space. We're hidden too far back in the building. It's too hard to escape. We have to run past all those people in the lobby. Anyone could see us."

Nathan removed a 9mm from his coat pocket and dropped it on the table. Next to it, he placed a noise suppressor. "These walls are thick. No one is going to hear us, and when we're done, we go straight out the back. You, me, Everett and his guys, and Alec. Together. You really worry too much. Besides, we're only going to be here long enough to meet up and then we head for the gondola."

"I still don't like it. We should have them meet us up there. It's better stocked, anyway. More secluded."

"If they meet us at The 10th," Nathan said, "we give up control of the scene. What if they get there early and decide they don't like the space? What if they demand to meet somewhere else? This way, we all get on the gondola so we can all go in at the same time. Cops are suspicious by nature."

"So?"

"This makes them feel like they have control. Looks like an even playing field. And then we can lead them into the south entrance, right where we want to go. Abandoning that plan would be an emergency-only situation."

"Alec isn't here, but he was supposed to be here hours ago. I think this qualifies as an emergency."

Nathan gritted his teeth and hid his pistol and noise suppressor. Wasn't sure if agreed with Zaluski or not.

# CHAPTER THIRTY-SEVEN

EVERETT WELKER CRANED his head as two lovely young ladies in skinny jeans passed him in the Lionshead area of Vail. He watched their butt cheeks swish back and forth in jeans so tight they looked painted on. He liked the idea that he'd have to struggle to peel them off those slender legs. Everett liked a challenge.

"My, my," he muttered to himself. He hadn't been to Vail in a long time, in what seemed like decades. The ski bunnies no longer wore spandex and Ray Bans. Hell, they weren't even *ski* bunnies anymore. All the young people snowboarded now, wearing those brightly-colored helmets with the tiny video cameras on top. Because everything they did in their lives needed to be recorded, edited, and shared online.

Everett turned his head back to the street in time to avoid bumping into some waif-like Arabic man with a beard obscuring most of his face. They made eye contact for a split second, but it was long enough for Everett to form an opinion.

Instinct told him to follow the man, but Everett was headed in the other direction. He had a meeting in one hour at the other end of this tiny town, and he wanted to grab a coffee first. Couldn't walk into a meeting like this feeling all drag-ass.

Plus he had to convene with his partners before meeting Zaluski and the Auerbach brothers. No way would he let those three outnumber him, despite whatever promises they'd made. People in this line of business were always looking for a way to cut out any chokepoints, because it's always about *money money money*.

Everett picked up a coffee and headed toward the covered bridge, and he paused when Mountain Haus came into view. Something about the building made him feel uneasy.

Instead of crossing over the bridge, he walked down to the bank of the creek and sat in the remnants of the last snow. Frozen rocks stung his ass as he settled. He sipped the coffee while he stared at the condo building where he was to meet his prospective new business partners. For some reason, they wanted to meet here and then take a gondola ride together up the hill. That in itself felt strange. Why not meet at mid-mountain?

The circular courtyard in front of the condo building was quiet.

No sign of Nathan or Alec.

He didn't trust those damn Polacks to do anything besides try to screw him out of his share. But, if he suspected they were going to weasel out of cutting him in on the airport action, he could slap the cuffs on them and be done with it. One clear advantage they didn't have, that was for sure. They could claim he was involved all they wanted, but the Auerbachs had no proof. They had only their word, which wasn't worth shit in the interrogation room.

But he suspected that the more likely outcome was that they were going to draw their guns on him. And that's why, in addition to Everett's two visible partners, he was going to have two more waiting in the wings, ready to put those bastards in the ground, if the need arose.

If he killed them, it would make it harder to take over the business, because he didn't know their distributor. They had all the leverage there. So Everett would play nice, as long as things were going his way. The second it stopped, he would turn that meeting room into a bloodbath.

He rose from his spot on the bank and scurried off to find a trash can for his empty coffee cup.

∼

Micah opened the heavy glass door of Mountain Haus, let Frank enter first. The inside of the hotel was carved stone and fireplaces, earth-tones everywhere. Like a mix of ski lodge and yoga studio. The building was a "full service" condo; even though people owned the residences, there was still a concierge, spa, rooms for meetings.

Micah had attended his first AA conference here, six months ago. He'd been surprised to learn how rowdy a bunch of sober drunks could be when they were all in a place like this together. Everyone running around with their name tags on like *Recovering Alcoholics Gone Wild,* except without the fuel of booze.

Micah and Frank paused inside the door, studying the lobby's layout.

"Think they're going to gather in their room?" Micah said.

"Could be. Or could be in a meeting space, like one of the conference rooms."

"Seems strange. It's almost too public."

A young woman stood behind a curved wooden desk, and Micah threw on a beaming smile as he approached her. "Hi."

The girl smiled back, a little flirty but professional. "Afternoon, sir. Welcome to Mountain Haus."

"I was hoping you could help me. I'm meeting two of my associates from out of town here. It's for a business meeting, but I'm not sure which room they're in. Can you help me with that?"

She raised an eyebrow. "Could you tell me their names?"

"Auerbach and Zaluski. One guy's tall with dark hair, the other one is severely European with a shaved head. I mean, he looks like he might be right at home in a tracksuit, if you know what I'm saying."

She tilted her face and wrinkled her nose. Evidently, she did *not* know what he was saying.

"Has some cuts on his face. Is this ringing any bells?"

Her hands hovered over the computer's keyboard, but she wasn't typing anything. She was going to need more.

Frank joined Micah at the reception desk. "They might have reserved a conference room, possibly?"

Her face lit up. "Oh, right. Twin Engine Experience. Yes, they've got some kind of company summit in conference room B. My apologies, sir, I didn't recognize the names."

"B," Micah said. He thanked her and eased passed the desk, toward the elevators. A sign indicated room B to the left. Once they'd turned the corner, they found themselves in an empty hallway. Micah slipped a hand into his jacket and gripped the taser gun. Frank also took his 9mm from his holster and held it inside the flap of his jacket.

"When we came here for the Area conference," Micah said, "did you think you'd be back in a few months with a loaded gun?"

Frank grinned. "Never say never."

Micah stopped outside the door. Nodded at Frank. Pushed the door open.

To an empty room.

"What the hell?" Frank said.

Micah noted that several of the chairs near the conference table weren't neatly arranged around the edge. One of them sat against a back corner of the room. Fingerprints on the glossy shine of the conference table's finish.

Someone had been in here at some point today, after the room had been cleaned last.

Frank pointed at a tissue on the seat of a chair, used and wadded up. A hint of blood on the tissue.

"What do we do, Frank? Do we wait? Do we find somewhere nearby and keep an eye on the entrances and exits?"

"Let me think a second." Frank walked the perimeter of the room until he accidentally kicked something that pinged off his shoe. The object skittered across the carpet and landed at Micah's feet.

A little glass device that Micah recognized as a *bullet,* or what some people called a *sniffer*. Big enough to hold at least a sixteenth of coke, maybe more. Micah hadn't seen one of those in years. Perfect for clandestine nose toots in the bar.

"Maybe they got spooked," Frank said. He pointed at the bullet. "If this is what they're fueling themselves with."

"I don't know. I can't believe they would have left town. After all the cloak and dagger to make this meeting happen?"

"We can go back to the parking garage and check. If we find their cars gone, we're back to square one."

Micah shook his head. "No, they're still here. But something isn't right about this meeting. I can't put my finger on it, but this whole Mountain Haus setup feels wrong."

CHAPTER THIRTY-EIGHT

G AVIN BELMONT SHUDDERED as he stepped out of his car in the Vail Village parking garage. He'd never enjoyed Denver weather, and had actually preferred the oceanic cool of Maryland and Virginia. But, Denver was tropical compared to Colorado's mountains. It was only October, but it couldn't be more than twenty degrees outside. How did the people in these mountain towns endure nine months of snow every year? Gavin would go crazy if he couldn't wear t-shirts and shorts on the weekends, couldn't get out on the open sea and feel the warm sun on his face.

He made sure to grab his US Marshal badge and service weapon before locking his car. Trusting Micah's hunch and a couple of easily-photoshopped pictures might turn out to be a huge mistake, but something in Gavin wanted to believe the guy.

Micah's first year in Denver, he'd been a mess. Gavin

had tried to help him, to keep him on the path to learning how to cope with living anonymously as Micah Reed, instead of as Michael McBriar. For most people it wasn't easy. Give up the person you've been for twenty, thirty, forty years? Takes days of practice sometimes just to make people respond to their new names.

Gavin had wanted the kid to succeed. Taken him on as a personal project, even though he wasn't necessarily obligated to devote as much time to Micah as he had. Some Marshals gave WitSec entrants their new docs and a little starting-off money, then rode away, never to be seen again.

But Micah had kept relapsing back into drinking, always on the verge of losing his job with Frank, not accepting his new life and identity. Gavin felt terrible about that part because he'd known Frank forever, and had persuaded Frank to take on Micah as an assistant.

Even though he wouldn't admit it out loud, Gavin had been relieved when Micah had dropped out of WitSec. But even more astounding, had found some way to get sober that had—so far—been a lasting deal. And Gavin supposed that's why he was here in Vail, paying a steep $20 to park in this concrete building, because some part of him wanted to believe that Micah had changed.

Gavin left the parking garage and took stock of Vail Village. Big hotel or condo complex immediately to his left named Mountain Haus. Circular brick courtyard out front. Little garden with some bronze statues. Next to that, a wooden covered bridge leading across a creek, still not quite frozen all the way. Beyond the bridge were shops and hordes of people.

Were they here to ski? With the setting sun, he couldn't see the mountains all that well, but the strips of bare mountain between the trees didn't look snowy enough for skiing.

Didn't matter why they were here, though. Gavin had to figure out why the hell *he* was here.

He walked across a courtyard and paused at the covered bridge. He sighed, since he had no idea where he was supposed to look, or what to look for. It wasn't too late to head back to Denver and book a red-eye to Dulles. Eat breakfast with his kids tomorrow, instead of eggs and hash browns at some overpriced Vail diner.

He cinched his wool coat tight. Maybe coming here had been a mistake, after all.

∼

At the top of the parking garage, Everett Welker crouched and scooted closer to the barrier. He pulled his fleece skullcap down over his ears as the sun started to dip behind the mountains. The cold was coming on like a freight train.

Something across the courtyard didn't look right.

He held a hand out behind him. "Toss me those binoculars."

His four associates crouched, peering over the three-foot wall at the edge of the parking garage roof. Clifton, the cop holding the binoculars, placed them in Everett's hand.

Everett focused on a man standing next to the covered bridge at the edge of the courtyard. Was getting harder by the second to see through this fading light. The man was wearing a long wool coat. Eyes darting left and right.

This guy was not a tourist.

Everett beckoned Clifton to scoot closer to him so he could get a better look. He passed the binoculars. "By the covered bridge. Eleven o'clock. What do you see?"

Clifton made a guttural *hmmm* sound. "Cop. Most definitely."

"Is he one of ours? Doesn't look familiar to me."

Clifton shook his head. "Never seen him before, boss."

"Son of a bitch." Everett slapped the concrete barrier with his open palm. The cold stung his hand like the smack of a rubber band. "Any of you seen this guy before?"

The other three took turns spying through the binoculars, each one of them shaking his head afterward.

"What do you think?" Clifton said. "Local or fed?"

Everett took another look, watching the man in the wool coat lift a cell phone to his ear as he turned onto the covered bridge and walked away from Mountain Haus. What he actually thought was that those grimy Polacks, Zaluski and the Auerbach twins, had sold him out. They'd brought in the feds so they wouldn't have to give Everett and his partners a bigger piece of the organ trade.

How would they swing it? Had Zaluski been wearing a wire during their conversation under the bridge back in Frisco the other day? Everett racked his brain to recall if he'd said anything incriminating during that brief meeting. He didn't think so.

Maybe this guy wasn't a fed. He could be some random cop from Colorado Springs or Durango, here as a favor to Nathan. Maybe they were planning to bring in this guy as leverage in the negotiations for the airport business. Claim this other cop was going to give them a better price for his services than Everett was asking. Get Everett to lowball his price.

Whoever the guy was, he wasn't part of the plan. The Auerbach brothers were trying to pull some shit, thinking Everett wouldn't be able to see the scam right in front of his eyes. But he wasn't going to let this slip by without doing something about it.

He said, "Clifton, you go down there and check it out. Take one of our guys with you. Go look at our meeting space and find out if our contacts are still there. If anything is strange, kill those ashholes, and kill anyone else who gets in your way."

CHAPTER THIRTY-NINE

ICAH SAT ACROSS from Frank at the conference table in meeting room B. Only five minutes had passed since they'd entered this room, but it had seemed like hours. They were no closer to discovering what to do next. Micah wasn't sure anymore why they were even here.

Frank wandered over to the window and looked out on the endless rows of condos wearing mountain peaks for hats. Living room lights flickered down on the town.

"Think they're coming back?" Frank said.

"I do."

"Maybe we set up on either side of the door, snatch them when they walk in."

"Not sure what good that does us, though," Micah said. "You can apprehend Zaluski for missing his court appearance, but then Nathan walks away, hops on a plane, and he's gone."

"Fair point, kid. Maybe we need to be somewhere we

can watch from the outside. Then we bust in on their meeting after it's started. But even that won't help if there's no hard evidence. This is a shitty hand we've been dealt."

Micah's phone rang, but he ignored it. It buzzed against his thigh, and he assumed it was some telemarketer. He never answered numbers he didn't recognize. This call, though, he didn't bother to check the caller ID. Little busy right now. "Whatever we do, sitting here is not the answer."

"Right," Frank said. "Let's go. Get a better vantage point."

"Top of the parking garage?"

"Something like that."

Micah led as they walked toward the conference room exit. But, as he reached out a hand to grasp the doorknob, it opened inward at him.

Micah found himself staring at two men, one of them a little pudgy and balding, the other well-built, with a square jaw. For a second, no one did or said anything. Micah figured the look of surprise on his own face must have matched the looks on these two.

They weren't expecting to find him here. They were expecting to find Nathan, Alec, and Zaluski. Was it meeting time, or were these two a scouting party? Or a raiding party?

The brawny one reached a hand into his coat pocket, and Micah saw the butt of a pistol jutting from a shoulder holster. He shot out a fist to punch the guy in the forearm.

The guy jerked his hand away from the gun, and Micah reached into his back pocket for his taser.

He'd almost managed to pull it out when the brawny guy jabbed his knuckles into Micah's shoulders, knocking him back. The taser flew from his hands and tumbled onto the soft carpet of the meeting room. Out of reach.

As Micah stumbled backward, trying not to fall on his butt, he caught sight of Frank struggling to raise his gun. The pudgy one (*cops, they had to be cops*) cracked a right hook across Frank's jaw so suddenly that Frank's body twisted and flailed, landing on the edge of a conference chair.

His gun flew out of his grasp.

Frank grabbed at the chair and flung it toward the pudgy cop. It scooted across the carpet and hit him in the stomach, forcing him to bend over.

Micah regained his footing and leaped forward. Didn't know where his taser was, and he didn't have time to find it. The brawny cop would have that gun out in a second and could kill both of them with two quick yanks of the trigger.

As he sailed through the air, Micah tucked into a somersault. He pointed his body at the brawny cop's legs. He bowled into the man's knees before he'd had a chance to move out of the way.

The cop toppled over Micah's back, unintentionally pinning him. Micah scrambled to get free, but the cop's weight pressed down, a giant block of flesh keeping him locked in his somersault position.

A gunshot sounded. Deafening.

The noise in the room collapsed under the pressure of Micah's ringing ears. He felt the cop above him shifting his weight, and Micah struggled against his confinement but couldn't get his legs underneath him.

Micah looked up to see Frank and the pudgy cop wrestling for control of his gun. Bits of pulverized tile floating down from the ceiling like snow falling in the room. Beige flakes dotted Frank's gray hair like dandruff.

Micah turned onto his back, and the brawny cop was now kneeling on his chest. The cop saw his advantage, grinned, and swung a fist down on Micah's nose. Micah felt the whiff of the air as that meaty hand came crashing down on him.

His eyes instantly filled with tears. He could feel the cop rearing back to punch him again, so he wrenched his left shoulder up with all his might, and it shifted the cop enough off balance that he could get a hand up and grasp the guy's hip. Micah rolled his body as he pressed, knocking the cop to the side.

The cop landed on the floor, his head thudding against the metal base of a chair. Bleary-eyed, disoriented. That wouldn't last long.

Micah scrambled to his knees in a flash, and then whipped out one of the zip ties he was carrying in his back pocket. He grabbed one of the brawny cop's hands and pushed it up his back, a few inches away from breaking the guy's arm. Struggling, he the struggling man's face into the carpet. Micah pressed his knee on the guy's wrist to keep it in place, then grabbed one hand and pushed it next to the other. He looped the zip tie over the joined wrists and yanked it tight.

The brawny cop yelped and Micah jumped to his feet, then he grabbed a conference chair and slammed it into the cop's head. Now dazed, he quieted and closed his eyes.

Frank.

Micah spun to find his boss standing behind the pudgy cop, Frank's hands under the guy's armpits and laced behind his head. The cop was thrashing but couldn't break free. For now, at least. Frank was leaning back to keep the restrained man from throwing him forward.

"Little help here," Frank said, struggling to keep his leverage. He backed up to the wall, and the pudgy cop jabbed an elbow in Frank's gut. Frank moaned but didn't let go.

Micah dropped to a knee and looped zip ties around the cop's ankles, then Frank wrenched the guy's hands into place so Micah could restrain his wrists.

The cop tried to get away, but with his ankles tied, the first step sent him crashing onto the floor, next to his buddy.

"Let's go," Micah said. People outside would have heard that gunshot. Nathan and Zaluski were probably on their way here, with backup. Micah and Frank had lost their element of surprise, so the only option was to flee and regroup. "Out of here, now."

Frank snatched his gun up off the floor and they dashed out of the room. A young couple cowered in the hallway nearby, the young man standing in front of the woman, shielding her.

"Get out of here!" Frank bellowed at them.

Micah and Frank sprinted along the hall, back toward the lobby. Micah heard Frank wheezing, but the old man didn't slow down.

Micah's phone rang again, and without thinking, he yanked it from his pocket and answered it.

"Hello?"

"Micah, it's Gavin Belmont. I wasn't going to come, but I started thinking about—"

"Wait, what? Going to come?" Micah rounded the corner in the lobby to find a dozen or more people standing around, looking concerned, asking each other what they had heard. But no Nathan. No Zaluski. "You're in Vail?"

"I am. I'm out walking through Vail Village right now."

"We're at Mountain Haus."

"Really? I was just over there."

"Get your ass back here," Micah shouted. "It's happening, right now. It's all about to get real messy if we don't do something to stop it."

CHAPTER FORTY

A CROSS THE STREET from Mountain Haus, nestled in the shelter of the bus stop, Nathan and Zaluski watched it all happen. Two of those plainclothes police officers had come out of the parking garage and entered the condo building. Nathan might not have even realized they were cops if one of them hadn't adjusted his jacket, which briefly exposed the badge clipped to his belt.

These were not cops Nathan knew. Had to be Everett's men.

Nathan's pocket buzzed and he fished out his phone.

"Yep."

"Nathan, it's me."

Took Nathan a second to recognize Scott's voice. Scott worked in logistics at the company in Broomfield, one of the few people who knew what was going on in that boarded-up side warehouse. Nathan hated to involve outsiders in the organization, but Scott had been instrumental in keeping the space private. Someone local who was full-time and could keep an eye on things. Plus, keeping him quiet was inexpensive, which Nathan appreciated.

"What's up?" Nathan said. "Make it quick, please. This isn't a good time."

"I wouldn't call unless it was important, Nate. It's the warehouse."

Nathan felt his chest tighten. "Go on."

"Everything is falling apart. Someone got in there last night, stole all the product, called the cops. There were detectives, crime scene people, reporters. It's all a big mess."

Nathan leaned forward and gripped his forehead with his free hand.

"What is it?" Zaluski said.

Nathan waved him off. "What do they know?"

"I'm not sure," Scott said. "I haven't been able to find out much. But I haven't told you the worst part. It's Alec."

"What about Alec?"

"I don't know how to tell you this. Your brother… he was near the warehouse. Someone stabbed him to death and then dumped him there. Doused him with bleach. I'm so sorry, Nate."

Nathan's mouth grew suddenly dry. A throbbing ache came from behind his eyes and made him woozy. He drew several deep breaths to keep from passing out. "I see. Is there anything else you can tell me?"

"That's all I know."

Nathan hung up the phone, then he let it slip out of his

hand and fall to the ground in front of the park bench. The clattering sounded far away, like an echo.

"What's going on?" Zaluski said.

Nathan leaned forward and picked up his phone. "We're screwed, that's what's going on. They sold us out. You were right about Alec. You were right the whole time."

"Alec was arrested?"

"No," Nathan said. "He's dead."

"What do we do?"

Before Nathan could answer, an old black man and a younger white man came sprinting out of the front of Mountain Haus. Running like someone was after them. Probably those cops who had gone in a few minutes before.

In a moment, Nathan recognized the white guy. Micah Reed.

But Alec was supposed to have taken care of Micah. And that meant if Micah was here instead, then he had killed Alec. He had probably surprised Alec, murdered him, and then ditched his body at the warehouse to tie the whole thing to Nathan.

Micah was at the heart of this betrayal, not Everett and his cop buddies. Micah had killed Nathan's only brother.

Micah.

This Micah was the one who had invaded his surgical room at the warehouse in Broomfield and had turned it over to the police. Had to be. The room Nathan had spent years developing, outfitting, securing. And in one night, this shithead had ruined it.

Nathan wanted to scream, to run, to tear Micah's head

from his neck. Instead, he gritted his teeth and forced himself to calm down. Think. He needed to think.

Zaluski grabbed Nathan's arm. "There. That's the cock-sucker who attacked me by the hangar. Let's kill that piece of shit."

"No," Nathan said. "Not yet. We need to get up to The 10th on the mountain. Get our guns. Then we come back and we will kill those two, and Welker, and all of these sons of bitches."

# CHAPTER FORTY-ONE

ICAH SPOTTED ZALUSKI by the stubble of his shaved head, across the courtyard outside of Mountain Haus. Scratches from when they'd tussled outside the hangar still lined Zaluski's face like diagonal war paint. And he was with Nathan Auerbach, the man at the heart of all this, whom Micah still hadn't encountered in person yet.

Micah had met his twin brother, of course, had seen him die while slumped on his bathroom tile. Micah had transported his dead body across town to dump him near the warehouse in Broomfield.

Nathan was tall and handsome. Micah wouldn't have suspected him of anything strange, if he didn't know better. He and Zaluski were on the opposite end of the courtyard, weaving through a crowd, on a path to reach the covered bridge.

Looking at Nathan's face, Micah couldn't help but

picture Alec heaving those final breaths, before the light had gone out of him.

"There," Micah said, pointing. He grabbed the sleeve of Frank's jacket.

Micah still had four zip ties in his back pocket, enough to secure both of these bastards until Gavin could come back and take them into custody. Would Gavin have enough evidence to do that? Micah wasn't sure yet if he could tie Nathan to the surgery room.

Micah reached for his taser, but Frank put his hand on top of Micah's. "Too many people. Let's see where they're going. Get them alone."

Nathan bumped into a woman in the crowd and she said something to him. Micah couldn't hear it, but she waved her hands in angry slashes as she spoke. Nathan reacted by slipping a knife from his pocket and slicing the woman across the face.

Micah gasped.

The woman screamed and people around now took notice of the melee. The woman didn't appear gravely injured, but a streak of blood cascaded down her cheek. She stood, frozen, crying and wailing.

A man standing next to her took a swing at Nathan, who responded by ducking and then jumping back a step. The nearby arms of different people tried to grab Nathan, so he and Zaluski broke into a run.

"The bridge!" Micah shouted.

Frank lumbered left, toward the covered bridge. Nathan saw this, growled something at Zaluski, and the two of them changed course. Now they were headed down the bank of the creek.

Micah waved at Frank and they both raced after Nathan and Zaluski. Even though the creek was low, trying to cross that water was going to slow them down.

Nathan plunged into the creek, splashing as he high-stepped through the water. Zaluski was on his heels. Chunks of ice cracked and floated downstream. By the time Micah reached the water, they were already on the other side, onto Bridge Street.

Micah changed course and raced back up the bank and thundered onto the covered bridge. Frank was close behind, huffing and puffing to keep up. The wooden structure rumbled with their heavy footfalls.

On the other side of the bridge, a uniformed officer emerged from a shop and held up a hand, barking at Nathan.

Nathan drew his pistol and shot the cop in the chest. The officer crumpled into a heap on the ground. Pedestrians everywhere began clambering to flee of the immediate area. Some people dropped into a crouch or went prone in the street. The little faux-European village turned into a madhouse of blurred clothing. Shouts and screams from all directions.

Micah emerged from the other side of the bridge, but with the flurry of people, he could no longer find Nathan among them. Like a marathon finish line where everyone was running in a different direction.

Micah paused, chest heaving. Lungs burned from the

frigid air. Frank came to a stop next to him, violently coughing.

"I lost them," Micah said.

Frank squinted at the crowd. Lifted a finger at the haphazard mess. "There," he said, pointing at Zaluski, sprinting toward a roundabout and turning left.

Why weren't they returning to the parking garage?

"The gondola," Micah said. "They're trying to get up the mountain."

Micah and Frank struggled to find a path through the moving organism of the crowd. Once they'd made it to the roundabout to follow toward the gondola, Frank reached into his jacket pocket and pulled out a folded baseball cap, which he slipped onto his head and pulled low.

"What are you doing?" Micah said.

Frank pointed across the roundabout at three men, also racing toward the gondola. "Cops. But not the kind on our side. Those are Welker's men."

Micah didn't know who Welker was, but he could tell these cops weren't here to arrest someone. The three men were all brandishing semiauto Beretta 9mms—pointed up and ready to fire—as they disappeared between the buildings. Micah gripped the hilt of his stun gun and Frank readied his own pistol.

When they rounded the corner, a few hundred feet from the gondola, they found Nathan and Zaluski racing toward it. Gondola cars coming on the return trip down the mountain slowed as they circled the base of the lift, their doors automatically opening as they passed through the loading station.

A Liftie standing at the gondola operator's station was waving his hands.

"We're shutting down for the evening, guys," the Liftie shouted. "Last ride was five minutes ago."

Zaluski raised his pistol and shot the Liftie in the head. He spun, then he plummeted face-first into the ground. His body didn't even twitch once he was on the ground. Dead before he'd started to fall.

Nathan and Zaluski jumped into a gondola car as it slowed. As the doors were shutting, they opened fire at the cops in pursuit of them. They immediately shot two of the police officers in mid-stride, which sent them tumbling to the ground. The remaining cop ducked behind a bronze statue of a skier in mid-turn. He peered out around it, but the gondola was already off the ground. He fired a single shot, which pinged harmlessly off the metal base of the gondola car.

Micah set his sights on the still-moving gondola. If he hurried, he could board the next one. That was as close as he would get until the next unloading station, halfway up the mountain.

As they neared the cop, the guy turned and lifted his pistol at Frank. Frank reared back and punched the cop in the face before he could get off his shot. The cop keeled over, his head banging against the base of the statue.

Micah and Frank reach the gondola loading station as the next cabin came around the loop. Micah hopped in through the open glass door, and he spun to reach for Frank. Yanked on Frank's hand to bring him inside in time before the doors automatically shut.

"Who was that?" Micah said.

Frank wheezed, trying to catch his breath. "Everett Welker. Piece of shit detective I used to know, back in Denver. He was supposed to meet those two at Mountain Haus."

Micah looked ahead at the cabin in front of them, two hundred feet up the cable. Each gondola like an enclosed ski lift chair, anchored to a static spot on the ascending line.

Nathan and Zaluski, standing, glaring smugly down at Micah.

"What do you think their plan is?" Micah said.

Frank coughed for a few seconds before answering. "Can't be escape, that's for sure. Wouldn't make sense for them to go up the mountain to get away."

"Then they have to have backup up there, or something like that. Some kind of failsafe plan in case the meeting at Mountain Haus didn't go well. Maybe they have more men waiting, or a stash of guns, or maybe they're going to grab snowmobiles and disappear over the mountain."

"Whatever it is," Frank said, "it would be better to find a way to not let them de-board."

Micah peered through the glass, down at the mountain. The gondola route would take them up and over the ski runs, sometimes as close as thirty feet from the ground, sometimes two or three times that high.

Micah looked back to the base of the mountain, at Everett Welker standing next to the statue. Gavin Belmont came racing up behind Everett, then he stopped, and the two of them shook hands. Everett had a pistol hidden behind his back.

"Damn it," Micah said.

"What?"

"Our only backup is about to be murdered by your piece of shit detective."

## CHAPTER FORTY-TWO

GAVIN COUNTED THREE dead bodies on his path toward the gondola. It had been easy to find; he followed the gunshots and the screams. Two of those bodies were in the cobblestone courtyard before the gondola. The third looked like a lift operator, face down at the gondola loading station.

A man stood next to a bronze statue of a skier, rubbing the back of his head. He looked up to see Gavin, then held up a folding wallet with a badge and ID inside.

"Everett Welker. Detective from Denver," he said as he put away his badge.

"What are you doing in Vail, Everett?"

Everett pointed at the gondola behind him. "Chasing those four who just got on. They killed two of my men, the sons of bitches."

Gavin noted that Everett had one hand behind his back. His lower lip was trembling. The warning Micah had given Gavin yesterday about *crooked cops* played in Gavin's head.

What was in that hidden hand?

"Who are you chasing, exactly?" Gavin said.

"Couple of hoodlums named Zaluski and Auerbach. Plus a bounty hunter named Frank Mueller and his crony."

Gavin looked up the gondola, trying not to show any reaction on his face at the mention of Frank's name. Gavin had known the old ex-cop for fifteen years. Had helped Micah get the job working for him after his relocation to Denver.

As the gondola continued to churn the cable up the slope, Gavin could see people in two of the cabins. He couldn't tell exactly who, because they were dots now, so far up the mountain. The little metal structures swayed gently back and forth, like wind-blown clothespins hanging from a laundry line.

Everett cleared his throat. "I didn't even know he was in on the whole thing until I saw him get on the gondola too. I can't prove if he shot the lift operator, but I have a suspicion it was him."

"This bounty hunter Mueller is part of this, is he?"

Everett nodded.

"Bullshit."

Everett swung his hand forward, revolver out. Gavin pivoted to the right and threw his hands out to grasp at Everett's wrists. His evasion removed him from the path of the gun, and when it fired, the bullet sailed past his chest. He felt his jacket ripple with the force of the air.

Gavin latched onto the gun and yanked on it as hard as

he could to pull Everett off balance. Everett tried to scramble backward to stay on his feet, but Gavin bore down, didn't give up his leverage.

He jerked the gun out of Everett's hands and continued the motion, leading Everett by the wrist so Gavin could position himself behind him.

Everett tried to spin out of his grasp, but Gavin had the leverage now. He pinned Everett's hand behind his back. With one foot, he swept Everett's leg to force him to the ground. Drove a knee into the crooked cop's back as he pulled the handcuffs from his back pocket.

"You have no grounds to do this," Everett said, grunting with his face on the ground.

"You pulled a gun on a US Marshal, you dipshit. You're lucky you're still alive."

As he slapped the cuffs on Everett, Gavin heard the sound of pistols cocking. He craned his neck behind him to see four uniformed officers, all of them with guns trained on him.

"Gavin Belmont, US Marshal. My ID is in my back pocket, so I'm going to reach for it."

The cops barked at him to do it slowly, and one of them approached to take it from his hand.

"Are you local?" Gavin said.

The officers nodded as they passed his ID back and forth.

"What's going on here? Did you kill these men?" the lead officer said.

Gavin shook his head. "I'm in pursuit of a fugitive who's now on the gondola." He pointed down at Everett.

"This man says he's a detective in Denver, but he tried to attack me."

Everett protested and the cops conferred with each other for a moment. This was all taking too long.

Before the cops could decide what to do next, Gavin listened to cracks of gunfire from up the mountain. Shots echoed down the side like thunder. Didn't seem like an excess of snow along the ski runs, but it might be enough to set off an avalanche. Gavin could see hikers moving through the trees.

Micah and Frank were in danger. He laid his eyes on a snowmobile parked at the base of the mountain. The snow was patchy in places and he hadn't ridden a snowmobile since a decade ago in Vermont, but it was the quickest way up that hill. If he stayed here long enough for these locals to figure out what to do next, it might be too late.

Without another word to the cops, he raced toward that snowmobile.

## CHAPTER FORTY-THREE

MICAH TOOK STOCK of the inside of the gondola cabin. It was about six feet by six feet, with two bench seats on opposite sides. The floor consisted of metal covered with rivets, and the windows and doors were glass with steel framing. From the bottom third up, the little cage was completely see-through, except for the metal roof.

And as he and Frank hurtled through space, rolling up the cable line toward the mid-mountain point where the next gondola loading station stood, he watched Nathan glaring back at him.

Nathan's arms were crossed and his eyes seemed to burn red.

Micah suspected Nathan had figured out his brother Alec was dead, and also that Micah had been there to see it happen. But that was crazy. Nathan couldn't know. He would have learned by now that Micah had raided his warehouse surgery room, no doubt about that. It had been

272

a full twenty-four hours since that whole mess in Broomfield. Micah had missed out on observing all the fallout since he'd left for Vail, but it had to be immense and far-reaching. Organ trafficking? Cops involved? Heads were probably rolling back in Denver.

Micah didn't have enough room to pace, so he sat and took Boba Fett from his pocket. Focused all his energy on the little plastic piece that constituted the space bounty hunter's head.

"We need a plan," Frank said. "We know they're armed. But a shootout up here is a bad idea."

Micah peered out the window of the gondola at some hikers trekking switchbacks through the snow up the mountain. Maybe those people hadn't heard the gunshots in town.

Frank passed a gun across to Micah. "Took this from one of those cops back at Mountain Haus."

Micah accepted the .38 Special, a snub-nose revolver. This little gun was reliable and had almost no kick. Not much stopping power, and not accurate at a distance, but it would get the job done at close range.

"I think the gondola unloads about halfway up the mountain."

"Problem is," Frank said, "they'll be unloading a half minute or so before we do. That's plenty of time to find cover and pick us off the second we step out onto the platform."

A gust of wind blew across the mountain, making the cabin rock slightly on the track. He thought of Gavin, facing off with Everett down the mountain. If Gavin was dead, that limited their options. Even if they survived, Micah and Frank might leave the mountain in handcuffs.

Micah studied the glass doors that would open automatically when they reached the loading station. A small metal bar stuck out from the side of the door. Emergency release switch.

"Here's what we do. When they're unloading, we'll be close. The gondola will be only five or ten feet off the ground as we near the platform. The second they hit that loading area, we pop open these doors and jump out. We'll be ready."

Frank frowned. "Won't be much good if I turn an ankle trying to leap out of this damn thing. Or if they have the same idea and get out early too. We're at a disadvantage, no matter how you slice it."

Frank was right, but Micah couldn't think of an easy alternative. At least for the next few minutes, all four of them were stuck in these two little cabins, not going anywhere but up.

Micah tried to clear his head and let the idea come to him. They were going to have to do something to gain the upper hand. No idea what, though.

And then, Micah looked up to see Zaluski leaning out of a window, pistol raised.

Micah grabbed Frank and pulled him down so they were out of view of the windows. Bullets pelted the glass, cracking it, but not shattering it. Four shots, five, six.

"This glass is thick," Frank said. "Might not even break."

The next few shots didn't hit the glass at all. Micah

raised up, got a look at Zaluski. Now he and Nathan both were firing, but their pistols were pointed slightly higher. Bullets pinged off something above the gondola car.

Where were they shooting?

Frank craned his neck up through the window, trying to see above them. "Son of a bitch."

Micah didn't have to ask. Nathan and Zaluski were shooting at the metal bar that joined Micah's gondola cabin to the wheels that ran along the cable. If they could hit a wheel, they might disconnect it from the track.

They were trying to detach the gondola car, to send Micah and Frank tumbling back down the mountain.

# CHAPTER FORTY-FOUR

WHILE NATHAN AND Zaluski kept firing at the thin metal bar keeping Micah and Frank's gondola cabin in the air, Micah scrambled to think of what to do next.

The gondola suddenly stopped moving, inertia making the cabin sway back and forth. There had to be cops at the bottom who had pulled the plug. Maybe Gavin had taken care of Everett and he'd stopped the gondola.

Either way, it likely meant the law was inbound. How long would it take police to get up here? Would they come up on snowmobiles?

If Micah and Frank could hold out a little longer, this problem might solve itself. Assuming the glass didn't crack and a bullet didn't ricochet into Micah's head as they hid on the floor of the gondola car.

And then, the shooting stopped. He poked his head up, found the two attackers standing there.

"What the hell happened?" Frank said, on the floor between the two benches.

"I think they ran out of ammo," Micah said.

"Perfect. Now we can shoot back." Frank scrambled to get to his feet, then he punched the emergency door release to open it. As he leaned out, Micah grabbed Frank's arm.

"Wait, Frank. Look down."

Micah pointed at a group of four hikers who were standing, fascinated, almost directly below them. Goggling like clueless children.

"Move out of the damn way!" Frank shouted. "Get out of here!"

The hikers looked up, waved. Maybe they hadn't seen the guns. Thought the shots were fireworks or something.

"Let's wait," Micah said. "Cops have to be on their way."

When Micah looked back up at Nathan's cabin, his mouth dropped open. Zaluski was climbing out of their open gondola door, then he lifted himself on top of it. He stripped off his jacket and spun his arms to coil the jacket around itself. He knelt and placed it on top of the cable, letting the jacket fold over so it hung down, half on each side, like a towel on a drying rack. Then he grabbed two handfuls of jacket and dropped off the gondola, holding on like some kind of zipline hitch.

He was going to slide down the cable to collide with their cabin.

"Oh, shit," Frank said.

Hikers be damned. Micah leaned out of the open door

and fired off three shots. All three missed as Zaluski was now a blur of motion.

He slid down the cable. He'd be at their car in less than five seconds. Micah held out a moment longer for Zaluski to get closer, then he squeezed the trigger three more times, emptying his revolver.

Again, all three missed. The gondola was swaying, Zaluski was moving. Too hard to aim.

"Any more ammo for my .38?" Micah said.

Frank shook his head.

"This is bad."

Zaluski slammed into the side of their gondola cabin, and wrapped his arms around it. He removed a machete hanging from a scabbard on his belt and started to pulled himself up.

Frank lifted his pistol, but before he could get off a clean shot, Zaluski scrambled up to the top of the cabin.

Out of view.

Micah then heard a clanging above them. "What the hell?"

It wasn't just clanging. Zaluski was hitting something with his machete. Micah could feel the vibrations coming through the roof.

Zaluski was trying to unhinge their cabin from the cable track. "He's trying to cut us loose."

"Is he bat-shit insane?" Frank said. "If we crash, he does too."

Micah peered out of the edge of the gondola. They were probably forty feet above the side of the mountain. In the gondola or out of it, this was a bad place to fall. The wind rushed by again, making the cabin sway side to side, and also bob up and down on the line.

The clanging persisted. "We have to do something," Micah said.

Frank held up a hand to protest, but Micah ignored him. He climbed out the open door and scrambled up the side of the gondola. Cold, biting wind slashed at his exposed head and neck as he climbed.

When he could see up to the top, he understood why Zaluski wasn't afraid. He had a rope tied around his waist, which was attached to a carabiner hooked onto the main cable.

And he was using a machete to dislodge the gondola wheels from the cable. There were three wheels that ran along the cable like a track. Zaluski had the machete between the cable and the wheels, working at separating them.

He managed to dislodge one, and the cable twanged like flicking a taut rubber band. The gondola cabin gave a painful creak and tilted toward the ground.

Zaluski briefly lost his balance, so Micah pulled himself on top of the gondola while his adversary was distracted.

Zaluski stopped what he was doing and sneered at Micah. "You broke my nose, asshole."

"You stole my Nuggets cap. It evens out."

Zaluski lunged, and Micah didn't have anywhere to flee on the six by six metal roof. Tethered to the cable by a carabiner, Zaluski could make any move he wanted without worrying. If Micah moved his feet, he might slip and tumble to his death. He felt like an idiot for leaving the stun gun back in the gondola below.

So he did the only thing he could: as Zaluski slashed with the machete blade, Micah raised his hands and attempted to swat it away. He managed to smack it with the back of his hand, and a searing pain sliced across his flesh. The blade had cut through his glove. He felt the coolness of the air meet the blood gathering in the cut.

Micah's deflection had pushed Zaluski's hands down and left his head exposed. Micah popped him in that broken nose.

Zaluski wailed, and Micah saw his chance. He tried to snatch the machete away, but instead, he only managed to knock it from Zaluski's hands. Good enough. It clanged onto the metal roof of the gondola and then disappeared off the edge.

Pain exploded across Micah's jaw as Zaluski cracked him with a right hook. He expected a left jab as a follow-up, so he pulled his head back a few inches and thrust his hands out to push Zaluski away.

Out of the corner of his eye, he saw something slither out of Nathan's gondola cabin, toward the ground. A length of rope. Then, Nathan climbing down that rope, scurrying toward the ground.

"Frank!" Micah said.

"I see it," Frank called back up. "There's a rope under one of these benches. We have one too. I'm going after him."

Micah didn't have time to worry about Frank now. He'd disarmed Zaluski, but the European still had the upper hand. Micah was running out of room to evade the attacks. If Zaluski was smart, he'd go for Micah's legs. Micah knew jumping to dodge a leg sweep would be too risky. Zaluski would also figure that out soon enough.

"You killed Alec," Zaluski said. "He was a good person and a good friend."

"You need better friends."

"I'm going to enjoy taking your life."

Then, as he dodged another right hook from Zaluski, Micah understood exactly what to do. Zaluski had clipped his carabiner to the *downhill* side of the gondola wheels. That had been a careless mistake.

Micah took a step to the right, making Zaluski counter, turning his back downhill. Micah had a flash of thought that he was about to do the most stupid thing he'd ever attempted in his entire life, and it would probably fail and he would tumble to the mountain where death would await him.

Then he told his brain to shut up and he lunged, wrapping his arms around Zaluski's waist and pushing him off the edge of the gondola. They sailed through the air, Zaluski's carabiner screeching along the cable as they hurtled toward the next gondola cabin, two hundred feet along the cable below them.

Zaluski flailed and punched at Micah's head, but Micah took the hits and wouldn't let go. He hugged Zaluski's midsection with every ounce of strength he had in him. Instinct and adrenaline had taken over and Micah felt only the whiff of freezing wind on his face.

In another half a second, they slammed into the

gondola cabin below them. With Zaluski involuntarily leading the downhill charge, his back took the brunt of the impact. He made no sound. Micah reached up to grab the metal frame of the cabin, and he noted that Zaluski's head had lolled forward. Dead, or unconscious.

Micah didn't care.

He transferred his weight onto the gondola and pressed the lever to open the door from the outside. Swung his body onto the floor. He'd only been airborne for about two seconds, but he felt much better with something solid under his feet.

Rope under the benches.

He lifted the bench lid and found a collection of equipment inside. Flare gun, granola bars, screwdriver set. And a long piece of brightly-colored rope knotted around a carabiner at one end.

Micah snatched the rope and hooked the carabiner to the hinge of the open door. He dropped the rope, and it barely ran long enough to reach the ground.

For the first time in fifteen or twenty seconds, he checked in on Frank. He and Nathan were facing off, standing on the angled side of the mountain.

Nathan was half Frank's age and probably had fifty pounds on him. Micah had to get to him, fast. Frank might have been an athlete back in his day, but he was way past that now. He might not last five seconds in an even fight with Nathan.

Frank raised his pistol but Nathan ducked and tackled Frank's legs. When they'd both staggered back to their feet, the gun was a few feet away, a black dot in the snow.

Climbing down the rope would take too long. Micah cinched his gloves tightly and wrapped them around the rope. It would burn his hands, but the gloves would take most of the friction. At least, he hoped they would.

A gun blast sounded.

Frank and Nathan were struggling to get control of the pistol.

The last thing Micah glimpsed before he plunged down the rope line was Nathan stealing Frank's gun away from him.

## CHAPTER FORTY-FIVE

A S MICAH SLID down the rope to meet the side of the mountain, he tried not to think about the burning of his hands. Tried not to think about the zip line cruise he'd taken. Without a doubt, that had been one of the craziest things he'd ever done in his entire life. He couldn't even reconcile what he knew of himself against the risk he'd taken not sixty seconds ago.

He had to keep one thing in mind: getting to Frank before Nathan could kill him.

When Micah hit the ground, he noticed several sounds at once. Above him, Zaluski shouting. Apparently, not so dead. Two hundred feet uphill on the mountain, Frank and Nathan fighting. And, from downhill, the whine of a single snowmobile. Then, a moment later, several snow-mobiles.

Micah looked up to see Nathan trying to force the nose of a pistol toward Frank's face. Frank had a hand on the barrel, blocking Nathan. The gun was six inches from Frank's head.

Micah tried to sprint, but the sloppy snow underfoot gave him little traction in his tennis shoes. His quads burned with the uphill effort.

Nathan looked downhill at Micah and jerked the 9mm out of Frank's hands. He pointed the gun in Micah's direction and squeezed the trigger.

Micah ducked but the bullet whizzed by, far to the right. A second shot followed. Micah turned in time to see Gavin Belmont on a snowmobile, then Gavin's body twisting, flying off the snowmobile. The snowmobile raced on alone for a hundred feet before crashing on its side.

Gavin tumbled into the snow but quickly rose to his feet, one hand clutching the opposite shoulder. He was too far away from the snowmobile now, so he ran up the mountain on the same path as Micah.

Micah lifted his eyes back up the slope to see Nathan trying to aim his pistol at Gavin. Frank jabbed his thumb into Nathan's eye, and both of them fell to the ground. The tumbled together, forty or fifty feet down the hill.

Micah was now only twenty feet away.

Frank was on top of Nathan, his hands around Nathan's throat. Nathan lifted the gun and pressed it against Frank's temple.

Micah willed his legs to climb faster.

Frank lifted a hand off Nathan's throat to divert the pistol and it fired a few inches from Frank's head.

Ten feet away.

Frank swatted at the gun, but couldn't wrestle it from

Nathan's grasp. Frank then head-butted him, but Nathan still didn't release the gun.

Micah's lungs burned. His hands were starting to scream with pain from the friction of the rope. The adrenaline was turning to mush.

Five feet away.

Micah planted a foot then drew back the other like a field goal kicker. With everything he had left in him, he launched his right foot at Nathan's head. Felt the nose of his shoe connect with Nathan's flesh, and Nathan's head snapping to the side.

Off balance, Micah landed in the snow and tumbled a few feet down the mountain.

Now Frank grabbed the gun, but it didn't matter, because Nathan was out cold. Frank slumped into a sit, pistol out, wheezing. He worked his jaw a few times as if he was trying to pop his ears.

Gavin arrived, panting, his shoulder bloody. "Frank," he said, then couldn't draw breath to say anything else.

Frank dug a finger into his ear, not noticing Gavin. "Son of a bitch pulled the trigger half an inch from my damn ear."

Frank stood, his gun pointed at Nathan, who was starting to stir. Frank swayed, eyes swimming. His head jerked, and he noticed Gavin standing next to him. Smiled a delirious grin.

"You okay?" Gavin said.

"Yeah, oh, sure. I'm great. Good to see you, Belmont." Frank leaned over and barfed up his steak. He wiped his mouth, and in a delirious voice, said, "how is the Marshal's service treating you?"

Micah rolled onto his stomach and pushed himself to his feet. Looked back down the hill at Zaluski, struggling to unlatch the carabiner above his head, like a fish caught on a line.

Frank stumbled and Gavin took the gun from him. That ultra-close gun blast seemed to have scrambled Frank's brain.

Gavin snapped his fingers in front of Frank's face. "You with us?"

"I'm okay," Frank said as he blinked a few times and then coughed a wet gurgle. "Got my bell rung a little bit."

"Frank," Micah said, and pointed back at Zaluski.

Frank grinned, threw an arm around Gavin's shoulder for support, and the two of them started down the mountain toward Zaluski.

Micah let the tension in his lungs blow out as the air filled with the sounds of local police arriving on their snowmobiles.

# EPILOGUE

In the movies, after the hero saves the damsel in distress, she wraps her arms around him and gives him a big smooch on the lips. Sometimes, they ride off into the sunset together.

Sitting in Daisy's apartment, staring at each other across her dinner table, it wasn't like that at all. No smooching. No plans to hop on a plane for a weekend beach getaway.

Micah had removed her problem. Nathan and Zaluski were both in custody. Alec was dead. No one was threatening her life anymore. But since Nathan owned this condo, she would probably have to move out. The police would seize it. Her now-criminal now-ex-boyfriend wouldn't be able to financially support her anymore.

And Micah had no idea if Gavin Belmont would actually take any action to help her with joint custody of her son. Micah hadn't said anything about it to Daisy because he didn't want to get her hopes up.

The lines of her face all angled downward. Her eyes looked puffy, probably from hours of crying. She seemed like a woman in mourning. He didn't blame her.

Micah's phone buzzed, and he read a text message from new friend Layne.

*FYI, made it to Cheyenne and my meeting just in time to land the biggest security client I've ever had. Sorry for the secrecy before, I couldn't tell anyone until the deal went through. You doing ok? Situation resolved?*

Micah considered replying, but he put his phone away instead. He'd catch up with Layne later.

On the table before each of them sat a plate of enchiladas. Daisy had barely touched hers. Micah wanted to eat, but the rope burns on his hands made holding utensils difficult.

"You not hungry?" she said.

He shrugged. Didn't want to ask her to feed him.

"What about cheesecake instead?" she said.

"Can you cut it into little bites?"

She glanced down at his hands, the bandages still wrapped around his palms. "Oh, of course. I didn't even think about that."

"It's no big deal."

She left the table and disappeared into the kitchen. He waited for a moment, not sure what to do. He hadn't known what to expect from this evening. A passionate romance to rise like a phoenix from the ashes of this debacle? No, not really. When she hadn't returned his texts after they'd slept together, he'd known it was a dead end.

But to see her so sad, so morose, was too awkward. He didn't know how to comfort her.

He joined her in the kitchen as she pulled a big block of cheesecake from her freezer and plopped it on the counter. She took a large carving knife from the drawer and started to cut the cheesecake into slices.

"I haven't been all-the-way truthful with you," she said.

Micah tensed his jaw. "Okay."

She pulled one of the slices of cheesecake aside and cut it into smaller pieces, working the knife quickly along the block. "It's just that... when I met you, I had these ideas about who you were. As a person, you know."

"Okay."

"And then things got out of hand. I learned that I was wrong about so many things. But some things were already set in motion, and that made it difficult."

"I don't understand."

She sighed. "I wanted to tell you before, but..."

Daisy trailed off as she started on the next piece of cheesecake, chopping it into smaller bits. Then the knife slipped. Her right hand pushed the knife between the first and second finger of her left hand, slicing through the groove.

Sounded exactly like driving a blade into a piece of chicken. Micah watched the knife split the webbing between her fingers into two halves before she'd even realized it was happening.

She screamed and shook her cut hand, which made

droplets of blood rain down all over the cubed bits of cheesecake.

Micah leaped into action. He snatched a dishtowel from next to the sink and pressed it into her hand. Daisy whimpered and stamped her foot on the kitchen floor.

"It's okay," he said. "Put pressure on it here. Do you have gauze or bandages? Hydrogen peroxide or anything we can clean this with?"

"Yes," she said, her shoulders hitching as she breathed. She looked down at the dish towel, at the blood seeping into it, the red patch slowly growing larger. "In my bathroom, under the sink."

Micah pressed her uncut hand over the dishtowel and left her there, sprinting down the hallway toward her bathroom. He threw back the door and then knelt down to open the cabinet under the sink.

As his hand reached out to grip the knob, he heard Daisy running down the hall. "Wait, Micah. Don't open the cabinet."

But his hand was already pulling it open. When his eyes adjusted to the limited light inside it, his mouth dropped open. Sitting next to a bottle of hydrogen peroxide was a metal flask, big enough for a pint. Curved to fit the angle of a person's hip.

And on the front of the flask, the monogrammed initials *MM*.

Michael McBriar.

This was *his* flask. Or, it had been. He hadn't seen this in years, not since he'd been a member of the American branch of Luis Velasquez's Sinaloa cartel in Oklahoma. Not since before the trial, before Witness Protection.

He lifted the flask. Held it in his hands. It felt like coming home, like a dirty secret kept locked for many years, now suddenly unleashed.

He turned to find Daisy hovering outside the bathroom, clutching her bleeding hand to her chest. Terror on her face.

"This flask," he said. "How did you get it?"

Her mouth opened, but she couldn't say anything. Her head slowly jiggled back and forth.

He studied the raised initials. MM. It couldn't be a coincidence. Had to be this same flask he carried in his pocket, always sloshing with liquid with every step he took.

"You know who I am," he said, feeling anger rise up from his stomach. He held out the flask. "Where did you get this?"

Her chest heaved. "Please don't hurt me."

"Hurt you? Tell me what the hell is going on here, Daisy."

"I thought there was something strange about you, when we talked in the building that day. The day I met you. No Facebook, no Twitter, no nothing. All those vague comments about Oklahoma. It was obvious you weren't who you said you were."

Micah looked back at the flask. Thought about the thousands of times he'd lifted it to his lips, let its contents numb his pain. "How did you get the flask?"

"Bought it online with Nathan's credit card. There's a

group of Witness Protection collectors who trade this stuff."

A cold chill gripped Micah's spine. "Witness Protection collectors?"

She winced. "I'm so sorry. I was angry."

"The blog. The Inside WitSec blog. That's you, isn't it?"

She nodded, tears streaming down her face. "You're not who you said you were, but I see now you're not who I thought you were, too. It's all a big mess in my brain."

"When you said you were going to unmask all those people in WitSec, you were talking about me? I was one of the people you were going to expose?"

She nodded again, said nothing.

"But you had sex with me. Invited me into your home to meet your son. Why would you do all that?"

She shrugged, now openly bawling. "I'm stupid. Like the danger. I shouldn't have let you meet Caden, but I couldn't turn you away when you showed up here. I didn't know you were coming by that day."

Micah dropped the flask on the counter behind him, and Daisy watched his hands as he slipped them into his pockets. Her chest pulsed, her lips curled down in fright.

"I'm not going to hurt you, Daisy. I don't know why you'd think that."

"Because I know what you did in the Sinaloa. I know all about it."

His head was swimming. "I don't get it. Why the blog?"

"I was angry. Wanted justice. Because my brother never got the chance you did. He never got to escape from the bad people, scot-free. He died because of people like you in the drug business. Yes, he sold drugs too, but if he'd had the chance you got, he could have become a good person. But we'll never know that now, will we?"

Her tears were like a knife puncturing his chest.

She assumed WitSec was the good life. She had no idea what he'd been through to get to where he was now, but he didn't want to argue with her. In a way, she was right. She had grounds to be angry. Micah had experienced the grungy side of existence and had lived to tell the tale. Lots of good people didn't get that chance. Maybe her brother was one of those people, but Micah couldn't do anything about that.

"I didn't even know you knew anything about computers," Micah said.

"I run a few websites to make a little money from the ads. My astrology blog is popular, but the WitSec one was also gaining traction."

"All those insider details, like the new names of people in the program. How did you know all that?"

"Some of it I got from articles on the internet."

"But not all of it. Those names are classified."

"Wait here," she said, and disappeared from the doorway.

In a moment, she returned, holding a black leather suitcase in her undamaged hand. She set the case on the floor.

"What's that?" Micah said.

"There was a Marshal named Kevin Neary. He died during a carjacking in DC a couple years ago, and this suitcase was in the trunk of the car when it was stolen.

The case made its way to the WitSec collector community, and I bought it. Well, with Nathan's money, but he didn't know."

Micah had never met anyone in the Marshal's service named Neary. "I don't get it."

Daisy sighed. "I spent weeks trying to figure out how to open the case. It had a keypad lock on it, but I finally stumbled on the combination. I was the first person to open the case since Neary died, as far as I know. Inside it was a manuscript, because Neary was writing memoirs about his time in WitSec. He was going to expose everything. But he died before he got that chance, so I did it for him."

Micah pointed at the suitcase. "Was my story in his manuscript?"

"Bits and pieces, but not your new name, so I put the rest together on my own. Meeting you that day sparked my whole interest in this thing. Secret people leading secret lives."

A darkness settled over Micah. If Daisy could figure out who he was, anyone could. His world felt fragile, teetering on the edge of a cliff.

"I trusted you," he said.

"You shouldn't have."

No one spoke for a few seconds, and the air between them felt thick, like soup.

"So what now?" she said. Her chest still heaving, her eyes still wide with fear.

He touched the flask with a fingertip. It was his, but he didn't want it anymore.

"Do you want me to bandage your hand?"

She shook her head.

"Do you want me to take you to the hospital?"

She shook her head again.

"Then I'm going to walk out the door, and I don't expect I'll see you after today."

She didn't seem to believe it. "I don't want you to be angry with me. I wrote those posts weeks ago and had them all scheduled in advance to publish on certain days over a span of a couple months. I did it before I'd even come to Frank's office."

"But then you did come ask for my help, even though you knew who I was."

"I wanted to find out for myself. Face the monster of the Sinaloa up close."

Micah gritted his teeth. "I'm sorry about what happened to your brother, but I didn't do that. I hope you'll decide not to publish my name on your blog. But I know I can't make you do anything. You should know, though, that if you expose me, it's not just me who'll suffer. I have a brother and a sister and both my parents who are still alive. The remaining Sinaloa people will come after them, too."

Daisy kept her head down, not meeting his gaze. He turned back to the cabinet and snatched a roll of bandages and the hydrogen peroxide, and then set them on the counter.

He walked to her, and she flinched back from him. He didn't understand how she could be so frightened of him, yet still spend time with him, pretending nothing was wrong. But maybe that explained why she'd been with Nathan in the first place. Her ability to be someone else when necessary.

Daisy the chameleon.

"Goodbye, Daisy. Please take care of yourself."

She still didn't lift her head.

He left her there and walked to her door. With his hand on the doorknob, he paused, trying to think of something to say to persuade her. He hoped she wouldn't publish a post exposing him.

But hoping was all he could do.

~

INSIDE WITSEC BLOG
SITE ACCESSED 10.23

*We're sorry, the blog you're looking for does not exist. If you feel this is an error, please contact our Technical Support department by using the Help link at the top right of this page.*

~

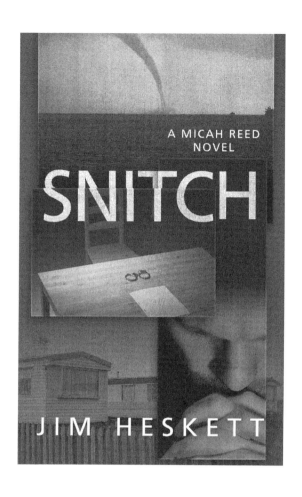

A MICAH REED NOVEL

SNITCH

JIM HESKETT

Ready for more? get the sequel SNITCH at
www.jimheskett.com/snitch

Ready to get the next book? The next one flashes back to Micah's time before the cartel and will answer many of your questions about the series!
Get SNITCH at www.jimheskett.com/snitch, the long-awaited prequel!

I've always been fascinated by gritty noir dramas, particularly the femme fatale brand of detective fiction. A sultry dame walks into the private investigator's office. He knows she's going to be trouble, but he can't help but give her aid, anyway. My intention in Blood Thief was to write a twist on that genre, because you don't really understand that Daisy is a femme fatale until the surprise at the end. But Micah should know better by now, shouldn't he?

If you started reading Micah Reed's adventure with this book, go back and take a peek at Airbag Scars. Micah's backstory will make a lot more sense. It's not available for sale on any platform, but you can get it FOR FREE on my website. Seriously.

With that out of the way, thank you for reading my book!

Please consider leaving reviews on Goodreads and wherever else you purchased this book (links to retailers at www.jimheskett.com/blood). It only takes a couple minutes, and you have no idea how much it will help the success of this book and my ability to write future books. That, sharing it on social media, and telling other people to read it.

Are you interested in joining a community of Jim Heskett fiction fans? Discuss the books with other people, including the author! Join for free at www.jimheskett.com/bookophile

I have a website where you can learn more about me and my other projects. Check me out at www.jimheskett.com

and sign up for reader group so you can stay informed on the latest news. You'll even get some freebies for signing up. You like free stuff, right?

*For Geneva Heskett, who cuts up the cheesecake.*

Published by Royal Arch Books

Www.RoyalArchBooks.com

Want the exclusive Micah Reed prequel novel for free? It's not available for sale anywhere, but you can go to my website for more information.

# ABOUT THE AUTHOR

Jim Heskett was born in the wilds of Oklahoma, raised by a pack of wolves with a station wagon and a membership card to the local public swimming pool. Just like the man in the John Denver song, he moved to Colorado in the summer of his 27th year, and never looked back. Aside from an extended break traveling the world, he hasn't let the Flatirons mountains out of his sight.

He fell in love with writing at the age of fourteen with a copy of Stephen King's The Shining. Poetry became his first outlet for teen angst, then later some terrible screen-plays, and eventually short and long fiction. In between, he worked a few careers that never quite tickled his creative toes, and hasn't ever forgotten about Stephen King. You can find him currently huddled over a laptop in an undisclosed location in Colorado, dreaming up ways to kill beloved characters.

He blogs at his own site and hosts the Indie Author Answers Podcast. You can also scour the internet to find the occasional guest post or podcast appearance. A curated list of media appearances can be found at www.jimheskett.com/media. He believes the huckleberry is the king of berries and refuses to be persuaded in any other direction.

If you'd like to ask a question or just to say hi, stop by the About page and fill out the contact form.

*More Info:*
www.jimheskett.com

Made in the USA
Lexington, KY
03 June 2019